BAD VAMPIRE

A CAT MCKENZIE NOVEL

LAUREN DAWES

BAD VAMPIRE

A CAT MCKENZIE NOVEL

And for Phil and Evie
...always.

1

orst. Day. Ever.

No, I wasn't being dramatic, although I had been accused of that on more than one occasion. Mostly by ex-boyfriends and blowhards who thought they knew me. Which, FYI, they *did not*.

"Are you even listening to me, Officer McKenzie?"

"Yes, Captain Wolfe, I am," I replied, meeting his steely gaze for a fleeting second. Even though he was sitting down, he still towered over me. At five foot four, I was used to having to crane my neck back to meet people's eyes, and most of the time, it was because they thought they could stare me down and intimidate me. Well, it didn't work for Peter Prince in elementary school, and it sure as shit wasn't going to fly now.

Besides, I had a gun and I was a damn good shot.

At least, I would once they re-issued it to me. Right now, it was staring at me from beside Wolfe's elbow, along with my badge.

"How was the week off?" he asked, leaning back in his chair, the steel frame creaking a little with the movement. "Been keeping busy?"

I glanced up briefly, then looked away. With blond hair buzzed close to his head and steely gray eyes, Vaile Wolfe had an aura about him that scared the pants off of me, and anything that scared me, I tried to give a wide berth. And avoided looking at.

If I could be in another zip code right now, I would be.

"Honestly? It sucked. Hard."

He smiled with more teeth than necessary, making the grin look malevolent. "You could've gotten out of town. Visited family?"

"I don't have any," I replied, trying not to fidget in my seat. When I fidgeted in my boss's presence, I felt like I was prey.

Heaving a sigh, he flipped open a folder and scanned the contents. "You've only been with us for eight days." Ah, so that was my career record then.

It felt like a statement I should have a rebuttal to, but it was the truth. Okay, so here's what happened—on my first day on the job, my partner and I got into some trouble. Yes, he was killed in front of me. Yes, I froze like a fucking deer in headlights…or like someone who just found out that all those monsters she'd been told *weren't* real, actually were.

"You've been on compassionate leave for seven days."

I held back my snarky reply.

Captain Wolfe was a scary motherfucker who didn't appreciate being interrupted.

I figured that one out for myself on day one.

'Compassionate leave' was a nice way to put it though. I'd watched my partner die a horrible, horrible death. And just stood there. Then they told me not to come into work for a week while they decided my fate.

"Are you still struggling with the Reveal?" Wolfe asked softly. "It's okay if you are. It's only been six months, but for many, adjusting to the new reality is hard."

The Reveal was the day the world found out humans weren't the only ones living on this planet.

It had all started with multi-billionaire John Davis and his shitheel son, Marcus. Marcus was convinced that dear old dad was running his auto-manufacturing company into the ground, and as a result, running all of his inheritance into the ground. The solution, in Marcus's mind, was to hire a hitman to get rid of his father. The hitman, as it turned out, was fae, and when Marcus was eventually arrested for conspiracy to commit murder, he sold the hitman out in order to save his own skin.

In a much-publicized trial, the hitman—a fae named Kailon Perry—took the slight to heart…and out on Marcus's ass. In front of the cameras, he let everyone see what he hid beneath his glamor while he tore Marcus Davis limb from limb. Literally.

After that, all the supernaturals had come out to play—and all of them were monsters as far as I was concerned.

I brushed away a piece of lint from my jeans and shrugged.

"I'm fine. I suspected we couldn't be the only ones out there, you know? Like aliens or an emotionally available man."

Vaile grunted and closed the folder, drumming his fingers on top of it. "So, what are we going to do with you?"

I braced myself with a deep inhale and closed my eyes. "Let me come back to work?"

Silence.

I peered at my boss and found him studying me.

"And what role would you have if you did?"

Please not a desk job. Please not a desk job. Pleasenotadeskjob. I wasn't content to just sit on my ass all day and push paper. I wanted to be out on the streets, catching bad guys and kicking the ass of anyone who didn't toe the justice line. "The same one?" My question came out slowly, monitoring how my boss felt about the concept.

He shook his head. "I don't think so, McKenzie." Leaning forward, he planted his elbows onto the blotter and said, "How about we play a game? I suggest something, and you tell me how you feel about that option."

Wow, that didn't sound so terrible. "Okay."

"PIG."

"I thought petty insults were below you, boss."

He gave me flat stare.

I shook my head. "No. And how? It's a department just for supes. If you haven't figured it out yet, I'm not a supe."

PIG was the very poorly selected, yet hilariously accurate, acronym for the Paranormal Investigative Group—a department made up of supernaturals who also happened to be cops before the world was turned upside down.

His smile was cold. "Human liaison. We need one for human on supe or supe on human crimes. The department has been requesting one for almost three months now. Guess who I selected for the position."

"I won't do it," I replied, not meeting his eyes. "I refuse. You can shove me behind a desk, or make me work reception. I'd even consider being your personal coffee bitch for all eternity, but not PIG."

His brows rose. "Coffee bitch, huh"

"It doesn't even have to be just coffee. I'd be your multi-purpose gopher. Need a gift for the little lady? I'll get it. Need a babysitter?" I thumbed my chest. "I'm your girl. I'll do whatever you want for however long you want, as long as I don't have to work with PIG."

"*The little lady*?" he asked. "I don't know whether to be insulted or amused. I know my wife wouldn't take too kindly to the moniker…but it's non-negotiable. You either accept you're working with PIG, or you'll be suspended without pay for six months *in addition to* mandatory therapy three times a week *and* a desk job when you return."

"You can't do that!"

"Oh, you think I'm bluffing?" Wolfe asked smugly, folding his arms over his chest. "Are you sure you want to find out?" When I stayed quiet, he added, "They're expecting you tomorrow morning at eight-thirty." He jabbed his finger at me. "Don't be late. Don't be an asshole, and for fuck's sake, don't get yourself killed."

"Myself? Not my partner?"

He snorted. "McKenzie, you'll be playing with the big boys, so if anyone is going to get themselves hurt, it's going to be you."

I opened my mouth, then closed it, and Wolfe's expression softened.

"It's a good deal, kid."

I tried not to let that 'kid' comment rankle, but it was really fucking hard.

"No one else in your department wants to work with you. They don't trust you to have their back. If you're serious about being a cop and keeping your job, this is your only option."

I looked him directly in the eyes, holding in check the shiver I felt tracking up my spine. "How long is this punishment?"

"At least twelve months."

Twelve months? How in the hell was I supposed to work with a group of people who I wouldn't trust at my back?

I swallowed, realization slamming into me like a bus. I was railing against something that everyone else in the department was railing about too, because that was exactly how my colleagues here felt about me. I'd let my partner get killed when I was supposed to have their back, and I'd done it all without lifting a goddamn finger. Fuck!

Why was life such a shitfight sometimes?

Peeling my back away from the chair, I stood up and waited as Wolfe slid my side arm and badge across the desk.

"Take the rest of the day off, but I'll be getting regular updates from Detective Taylor about your conduct once you start with PIG."

"Great," I deadpanned. There was nothing I liked more than micro-management. Sliding my side arm back into the underarm holster I wore under my jacket, I clipped it in, then put my badge back into its cover.

As I turned to leave, Wolfe added, "You're going to be a great cop, McKenzie."

I glanced over my shoulder. "And you know this, how?"

He touched the side of his nose. I rolled my eyes before pushing out of the office and into the din of ringing phones and the low hum of computer monitors that rarely got turned off. Navigating to my cubicle, I slumped down into my seat and stared at the workspace that had been mine for all of twenty-four hours.

I pulled open a drawer and reached inside, picking up the stray paperclip at the bottom. I sighed. I hadn't even gotten around to stealing office supplies yet. Leaning back, I let my gaze drift across the room, glaring defiantly at anyone who had the balls to stare. I already knew I was unpopular. Them staring would just put me in an even shittier mood.

Shouldering my bag, I stood up and walked out of the office, the noise of whispered conversations following me.

They didn't want me here? Well, fuck them. I didn't want to be here either.

2

"So, how are you feeling today, Cat?"

I studied Joanna Wong's face, wondering where to start. I'd been seeing my therapist for the better half of five years, not necessarily talking through the *real* issues, but rather skirting around them.

Her dark, almond-shaped eyes softened—the only feature she got from her Korean mother. Her dad was Caucasian with blond hair and blue eyes. I knew this because I snooped and saw a photograph of her and her parents on her desk. "Cat?"

"Can I say terrible?"

Joanna pursed her lips and recrossed her legs, her pressed pantsuit unwrinkled and obedient. "You can, yes, if that's how you're feeling."

Folding my legs up beneath me, I snuggled into the brown

leather couch. "I went into work today."

"And how was that for you?"

"It sucked," I replied, letting out a sigh. Being back at work only reminded me that I'd fucked up. I'd done the worst thing any rookie could do, and now I was paying for it. "I spoke to my boss."

"Is he letting you keep your job?" At my nod, Joanna added, "You don't appear to be too happy about that."

"I am happy...I think." I grimaced. Shit, speaking about my feelings had never been easy. I blamed it on my fucked-up childhood, where death seemed to just follow me around. I sat forward in my seat. "They want me to work with PIG."

"The paranormal department?"

I bobbed my head. "Yeah, because yay. You know how much I love the supes."

"Would you like to talk about your feelings when it comes to the supernatural world?"

"Not particularly."

She scratched down something on the notepad balanced on the arm of her chair, her two-carat wedding band winking in the light. "All right, so what would you like to talk about today?"

I shrugged. The truth was I didn't want to return to my empty apartment with my empty fridge and empty bed just yet.

Annnnd cue the violins. Fuck, I hadn't felt this sorry for myself in a long time.

"They want me to be the human liaison." Joanna stayed quiet, encouraging me to talk without using any words. I hated when she did that. I cleared my throat. "Why would they do that?"

"It seems to me that they're giving you a second chance."

"Yeah." Keeping my head down, because nobody likes looking their shortcomings in the face, I smoothed my hand over the cross-stitched cushion in my lap. "Look, I know I should be happy. I still have a job, but…"

"But how can you work with the supernaturals when you've got some strong feelings against them?" I grunted. Damn her and her Ivy League education. She pressed on, "Perhaps we can spend some time in the next session to discuss these feelings and how you've transferred them to your father's death in more detail?"

Oh, yes, let's rehash that one. I glanced at the clock on the wall above Joanna's head, relieved to see we'd reached the half hour. "Time's up." Discarding the cushion, I rose from the couch and stretched. "I have a kickboxing class to get to. It starts in an hour."

"You're still going? That's great." She smiled. "Well, I won't keep you. I'll see you next week."

"Thanks."

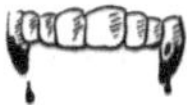

I WIPED THE SWEAT FROM MY BROW AS I SWUNG UP INTO ANOTHER crunch. The coach was a fucking demon tonight—figuratively, not literally. The class grunted out their count, but I couldn't find the spare oxygen needed to spit out the number.

"This guy needs to get laid," Sasha panted beside me as she

pulled up into her next crunch. "I call dibs."

I managed a grin. In between a grimace and a colorful swear word. "You're welcome to him," I replied, exhaling sharply through my mouth and wondering why I put myself through this torture.

"Come on…you can't tell me…you don't want to…fucking *ride* him…hard." Sasha had her hair piled up on top of her head like a poodle's, the tight, black curls holding their shape, despite the humidity in the gym.

"I'd rather his…head between my legs," I shot back, grinning when Sasha actually purred.

"All right, burpees!" Mike yelled in that sexy British accent he had. Sasha let out an erotic moan.

I did those burpees, and I did them with a fucking smile on my face. When Mike felt like he'd whipped us into enough of a moaning, aching heap, he asked one of his students to run a cool down and stretch session. As I lay in child's pose, stretching out my lower back, I leaned my head against the tacky blue mat and shut my eyes.

The opal necklace I'd been given by my dad, just after my mother died fourteen years ago, lay warm from my body heat against the underside of my chin, a comforting weight and a steady constant. I never took it off, even when I did this punishing class, because my dad had told me that it would always protect me.

I wasn't an idiot. I knew it didn't have magical powers. It was just that this was the last thing that he gave me and, stupidly, I felt connected to him through it.

With nothing else left to do, my mind began to work, the cogs twisting as I replayed all the horrible things that had happened today. Keeping my job was probably the least of the offensive things, but working with PIG? How in the hell was I supposed to pretend that I even liked these guys? In my head, they were the boogey man, that killer in the backseat, and Bloody Mary all rolled up into one. I was terrified of them, the irrational fear probably stemming from my father's gruesome and unsolved murder. His death had hit me hard, making me re-evaluate the art degree I'd been working toward at college and switching over to a BA in Law Enforcement.

Adding to my arsenic-laced shit sundae? Joanna Wong. How could she think this was going to be a good thing for me? For fuck's sake, I had a burning distrust of these beings, but if I was being honest with myself—let's face it, that's really no fun— then I also had an immense fear of the supernaturals. I'd seen first-hand what they were capable of doing, and if *that* incident put me into therapy, what would working with them every single day and investigating their crimes do to me?

Humans had long been the top of the food chain, or at least, we thought so. We had no natural predators, other than high cholesterol and cancer, but with supes on the scene now? Humanity certainly got knocked down a few fucking pegs. Fear was a heathly part of human evolution—that's how we'd survived for so long. But my fear had been amplified tenfold by my experiences of supernaturals, even before we knew they were real and not just monsters in the stories we were told.

As I pulled out of child's pose, I turned my head to find Sasha smiling at me.

"Want to go get pizza?"

I shook my head, shoving some of my loose aqua green hair from my eyes. "Not tonight. I had a shit day, and I was hoping an endorphin rush would help…"

Sasha huffed. "Please, girl. Looking at Mike in his tight MMA shorts helps every damn time."

I looked over at our instructor and found him smiling at me. I glanced away. "He'll be starring in my fantasies tonight."

"Girl, same." Sasha held out her fist for me to bump. "See you tomorrow?"

"Yup. I'm a glutton for punishment."

"Hashtag Masochist."

I laughed and stood up, stretching my arms above my head. "Hashtag You-Know-It."

Sasha sauntered away, and I went to retrieve my gloves and wraps from the edge of the mat.

"You're getting better."

I yelped, turning around with a hand resting against my lurching chest. "Fuck me, Mike. I'm going to have to put a fucking bell on you. You can't creep up on people like that."

More so because I was a cop and I was supposed to be aware of my environment at all times.

"Sorry." He grinned at me, popping a dimple I was helpless against. Every time I saw it, I went weak at the knees. "I just wanted to tell you that I can see your improvement. How long have you been coming here for?"

"Six months?" I wiped the sweat from my brow.

He nodded. "Six months, and you're already giving some of my full-time guys a run for their money."

I snorted. Yeah, like that was true. But I smiled graciously, because that was the kind of person I was. "Thank you."

"You got it." He looked over to the reception area, where the next class was waiting to start. I looked too, then frowned at what I saw.

"Supe class?"

"Yeah. One of my new trainers is a werewolf. He thought it might be good to start having separate classes for them, rather than mixing with the humans. They're all incredibly strong, and at least this way, they won't have to hold back."

"Do you participate in these sessions?"

Mike shook his head. "I'm strong, but these guys are in another league. I hear that they'll be starting an MMA cage fighting division just for supes. They can't compete with humans."

"More like we can't compete with them," I said bitterly. "How many do you have coming?"

"Every day? Maybe twenty. Some come every day, some only once a week."

"What flavor are they? Do you know?"

"From what I can tell, mostly shifters. Some vampires come, but there's bad blood between the two groups."

"Any fae?"

Mike shrugged. "Couldn't tell if there were. They look too human."

I grunted. I couldn't agree more with that. The fae were the ones that scared me the most. With shifters, there was a look in their eye, something predatory that gave them away. Vampires had fangs—*duh*—but the fae were difficult. The fact that they could use glamor too only made it worse. Were they all hideous? Is that why they covered themselves in 'human' skins? Whatever the reason, I had no way to detect who was who.

Sometimes, I wished those bastards would just disappear into the hole they crawled out of. The human authorities called the fae realm 'Wonderland,' which was cute if you liked the idea of one place where fae shed their skins and were every inch as badass as we thought they were. Wonderland wasn't something humans could access. We weren't even supposed to be able to see it, let alone set foot in it. And if we did? Instant death.

Yeah, the fae were a whole bunch of fun wrapped in barbed wire. They were the gift that kept on giving.

I waved goodbye to Mike, then stalked past the supes waiting for their class. One of them gave me the stink eye as I passed, and I returned the favor. I felt dirty even brushing past them. When I got to the front door of the gym, I stepped to the side to watch the start of the class.

Call me a glutton for punishment if you want, but there was something to be said about assessing the enemy.

The group began working through their warm-ups, each of them stretching out their powerful bodies in a weirdly synchronized way. Every single one of them—male and female—had muscles that bunched and flexed under their skin. They were predators in the purest form of the word.

They were dangerous.

With one final glare, I turned and left, wondering whether I'd just made the biggest mistake of my life by agreeing to join PIG. I guessed I'd find out tomorrow.

3

I woke up the next day feeling sore and irritable. Not only did I not sleep well, the idea that I was now an official member of PIG was making me want to scratch my own eyes out. As I got ready for work, I tried not to think about everything that could go wrong today. Talk about walking into a hostile workspace. The thing was, it was different from walking into a roomful of cops who were human. All they could do was talk.

Walking into a roomful of supes who had claws and fangs at their disposal? I had a feeling I'd find out how fast I could really run.

I stopped at the coffee shop to grab a shot of caffeinated courage before I made me way into the office. I scratched at my over-starched shirt and cursed that I had to wear the uniform again. Maybe the supes had a more relaxed dress code? That'd be amazing if it was true. I parked my truck and walked into the café, whistling softly as I did. The girl behind the counter gave me a warm smile.

"The usual?"

"Thanks, Jen." I paid for my order, then tucked a couple of bucks into the tip jar. I'd been coming to this place for about a year now, way before I'd joined the force, and while I was still in training too. Moving off to one side, I waited for my order, my eyes not focused on anything in particular.

My gaze rose when I heard someone with a dark, smoky voice place an order. I stared at the guy, unashamedly. He was tall—not hard when I'm rocking Oompa Loompa stature—with dark hair and crystal grey eyes. He was just the kind of guy I'd go for. All he had to have now was a twelve-inch dick.

Hey, a girl can dream.

My gaze drifted lower, to his strong hands that looked like he knew what to do with them. Like spank me when I needed it. Yeah, just thinking about it made me squirm. There was a breathy sigh, and I glanced over at the woman waiting two back in the line from him. Her eyes were on him too, the lust filling her gaze unmistakable, because I felt it as well. It was raw and strong and…

The necklace around my neck began to glow and pulse beneath my shirt. I glanced down at it, wrapping my hand around the stone to stop anyone else from seeing it glowing. What in the actual fuck? What was it doing?

The room seemed to pulse, like a breath held and not released, until finally there was a near audible *pop*. Somehow, I found the strength to tear my eyes away. I could still feel the pressure, the sexual desire dominating the space, but I didn't feel the need to scratch out the other woman's eyes with the stirring sticks at my elbow.

I looked at her again. She was stroking the base of her throat and the top of her breasts hidden beneath a lavender blouse. She was still under the influence of whatever the fuck was going down in this coffee shop. The guys didn't seem to be having the same reaction though.

The guy at the front of the line finally paid, then turned and looked at me right in the eyes. The necklace flared hotter again, and I flinched at the sudden surge of accompanying heat. It didn't burn, it was just uncomfortably warm against my palm, like a heat pack left against the skin for a little too long.

"Can I help you?" he asked smoothly.

He smelled of dark chocolate and whisky, and I found myself involuntarily licking my lips. Shaking my head, I focused on other facts, like everything about him was perfect, from the expensive haircut to his angular jaw and straight nose. Geez, even his teeth were perfect.

"Nope," I replied, smiling smugly when he looked a little put out that I wasn't floundering all over him like the other woman was.

Ha! Fooled him.

"Cat?" Jen called breathlessly, and I collected my order with a smile.

"I'll see you tomorrow, Jen."

The other woman's eyes fixed on the guy, and she nodded absently at me.

Okay, weird.

I left the coffee shop, feeling like I had a target painted on my back. It wasn't a target though—it was a set of cool gray eyes. Once I set foot outside, the heaviness in my pelvis began to ease. Clearly, I hadn't been affected as greatly as the other woman, but the relief was so great, I could've cried. I could only imagine how the other woman would feel once she stepped outside.

The guy had clearly been a supe, but what flavor? He looked human, but I didn't get that just stalked feel off of him, so not a shifter. Not a vamp either, because you know, it was eight in the morning. A fae, maybe? If he was, and he wasn't even trying to influence me just then, I didn't want to know what it felt like when he was actually concentrating on it.

I gunned my truck over to the station, bypassing my old department with a one-finger salute. Granted, where I was going now wasn't much better, but at least I didn't have to sit in a room full of people who hated me.

Seriously, it was like being back in high school.

Except now, all of these people were armed.

Wandering down the hallway, I sipped my coffee and kept my head down as I passed random people in the hall. Eventually, I reached the door with PIG written in big block letters on the front.

I took a moment to take a deep breath and let it out, then

opened up the door.

I fought the urge to walk right back out of there because… awkward. Everyone was staring at me. Everyone. And it wasn't the stares of your regular, run of the mill humans. It was the stare of predators. Keeping my chin up, I met each of their eyes, glancing away just at the right time. I didn't want to get into a fight with anyone…

At least not on the first day.

"Who are you?" a woman asked. She wasn't dressed in uniform, but rather, she was wearing a leather outfit that took BDSM wear to a whole new level. I wondered if that was standard issue for PIG.

"Officer Cat McKenzie," I replied, leaning up against a nearby desk. But when there was a low, dangerous growl from the owner of said desk, I straightened and stepped away. "Don't tell me that's what I have to wear to work."

BDSM actually hissed at me like a snake, her slitted eyes gleaming with promise. I'd found that since the supernatural cat had been let out of the bag, a lot of them stopped playing human altogether. They didn't even bother to hide what they were now.

"Why are you here, Cat McKenzie?" someone else asked. I searched the room for who had spoken, finding a human looking woman with dark hair and green eyes sitting at one of the dozen desks scattered around the room.

"Human liaison. Captain Wolfe sent me."

Someone snorted, then grumbled, "Like we'd need a fucking human to help us do our jobs."

"Be that as it may," I announced in my strongest voice, "I'm here." Although, who I was supposed to be working with, or in what capacity, I had no idea. "I was told to report to Detective Taylor," I added when nobody seemed to be offering up any other information or indicating who was running this shit show.

I tensed when I heard footsteps behind me, and I stepped to the side, watching the same guy from the coffee shop walk into the room. He had a cardboard tray filled with coffee cups in one hand, while in the other, he had a bag that smelled like it was full of pastries.

The guy glanced around, then looked at me. "Who's she?"

"Human liaison," someone answered. "Wolfe sent her."

"I'm Officer Cat McKenzie. Who are you?" I asked, finally finding my voice.

"Detective Taylor. Sawyer Taylor… and your new partner."

I tried not to let my eyes bulge out of my head on that one. "Partner?"

Sawyer offloaded his coffee tray and passed the paper bag to the guy who had growled when I leaned on his desk. "Partner. You know, those people who have your back and you have theirs? Oh! That's right," he said, slapping his palm against his thigh. I suddenly got a flash of him spanking my ass red, but shook the thought away just as quickly. "You're the one who watched her partner get torn apart by a demon last week."

His statement seemed to be a signal to the rest of the room, because along with the plunge in temperature, there was a rise in hostility. Cops who lost partners because of their own negligence were never trusted.

"Yes, the same one." I was glad my voice stayed steady. "You have something to say about it?"

Sawyer stepped closer, putting himself into my personal space. His face was so close that I felt the heat beading off his body, and his chocolate and whisky scent got tangled in my nose. I shouldn't have been enjoying this, but I was. Against my chest, my necklace heated in warning.

"Listen. I don't need a partner. You're only here as a fucking favor, and the minute you fuck it up, I'll be shipping you back for Wolfe to deal with. *In pieces.*"

"Well, aren't you just rainbows and unicorn farts in the morning," I drawled. "Look, Sawyer, is it? I don't want to be here any more than you want me to be here, but I have no choice. I'm still a cop, and this is what I have to do to get back on the job. So you do what you've got to, but we have to work together."

He grunted, running his eyes over me. "Human liaison, huh?" he spat, then turned on his heel, stalking farther into the room. I kept my breathing steady, even though my heart was racing. Sawyer moved to one of the desks in the back, and I followed him.

"Where do I sit?"

He waved his hand, indicating an empty desk to the left. "There."

With a nod, I put my bag down, shoved it under the desk with my foot, then sat in the office chair. Swiveling it around, I asked, "What kind of supe are you anyway? Fae? Demon? Nymph?"

He didn't reply, but the muscle in his jaw jumped.

When it became clear he wasn't going to give me an answer, I did a full revolution of my chair and asked, "So, what are we doing?"

He tapped angrily at his keyboard for a moment. Leaning over, I peered at his screen.

"Buxton Elementary School. You have kids that go there? I thought it was a human-only school."

Sawyer ground his teeth but didn't say anything more. Okay, he was the strong silent type. He continued to tap away, navigating his way to the 'staff' tab and scrolling through the faces of the teachers and aides. Eventually, he got to the end, then scrolled right back up again.

"You know, it might be more productive to slow down so you can actually read their names."

"I don't need to read their names," he said bluntly. "I just need to see their faces. Names are irrelevant right now."

I leaned back in my chair. "You are just so pleasant, aren't you?"

He rounded on me. "You want to see pleasant?" he snarled, his gray eyes darkening ever so slightly. "Keep asking me asinine questions, and I'll show you how pleasant I can be."

I narrowed my eyes at him, then shrugged. "Well sure, if you want me to keep going—"

"I don't!"

I peered around the room to find everyone watching us. I scratched my chin absently. "You know, I'm getting a lot of mixed signals from you here."

Sawyer's glare didn't ease up. If anything, it got a whole lot frostier. Abruptly, he stood up and said, "Come on. We have a case to work on."

I jumped up from my chair. "Oh, a case? What is it? Diamond heist? Corporate espionage? Sex club?"

That last one got me a raised eyebrow. What could I say? I had a healthy and curious sex life.

"We're going to the elementary school."

"I knew it."

Sawyer Taylor, meet sarcasm.

He rolled his eyes. "There was a report overnight of a baby vampire terrorizing some students backstage at a Thanksgiving concert."

I blinked. "I don't even know where to start with that one. There was a Thanksgiving concert last night, and *I* didn't know about it?"

Sawyer gave me another one of those sexy growls. "Let's go."

I expected him to lead the way out of the station, but he exited the office and hung a left instead. Producing a key from the inside of his pants pocket, he opened up a door in the long hall and stepped inside. As soon as he flicked on the light, I gasped. I couldn't look at just one thing, I wanted to look at *everything*.

"This is amazing," I breathed, reaching out to touch one of the sidearms nestled in its egg crate foam casing.

"Don't touch that!" Sawyer snarled.

I retracted my hand quickly. "Why?"

He snatched the weapon from where it was lying. "Because

you have no idea what this weapon does." He swept his arm wide. "What any of these weapons do."

I tried not to pout. Really, I did. "Let me guess, you aren't going to tell me either, because I'm some poor rookie cop who messed up like a puppy peeing on the rug."

"As much as that analogy fits you, no. The reason you can't touch any of these weapons is because they've been calibrated to specific species."

My brows rose. Wow. That was a new bit of information. I wondered whether Wolfe knew about all this tech. The room was literally stuffed with it.

"Okaaaay, so what *can* I touch?" I ran my gaze down his body until it settled on his ass, which was looking *fiiiiinnnne* in those tight slacks of his.

"No," he said, but without any conviction.

"No? No to what?"

A small smile pulled at the side of his mouth. "No to whatever you're thinking right now."

Around my neck, the necklace warmed. I popped my hip out and folded my arms across my chest. "How do you know what I was thinking about?"

"I can smell it."

I straightened, then looked away. Okay, that was straight up weird. What kind of supe was this guy? Clearing my throat, I wandered farther into the room, bending down to get a closer look at the weapons I couldn't touch. The technological evolution was maddeningly unfair. There were guns here that looked like they'd been props in the *Men in Black* movies. Hello, alien technology…or maybe just supe technology. Either way, it was badass.

"What are these?" I asked, pointing to a pair of handcuffs that were giving off a faint blue glow.

Sawyer appeared at my side. "Warded handcuffs that automatically adjust their size. They're designed to hold any supernatural creature, with the exception of gremlins."

I tried not to let that comment stun me, but color me stunned. "Say what now? Gremlins? Like the nasty green wart-ridden things in the movie?"

His mouth quirked up again, just a little. "Kind of. Just imagine them one hundred times bigger."

Holy shit. Gremlins were real?

"They're a kind of fae that doesn't usually leave Wonderland."

"Comforting. Really," I deadpanned. "What the fuck else is out there that I don't know about?"

He shrugged, and I admired the way his muscular shoulders moved under his shirt. So sue me. He had a fucking fantastic body. "Every book that's been written about the fae and creatures that go bump in the night is real. All of it."

I felt like the rug hadn't just been pulled out from under me, but lit on fire too. Every single creature was real? I didn't know whether to scream, cry, or lock myself into a bomb shelter and rock myself in the corner.

Sawyer plucked the cuffs from the case and handed them to me. "These are safe to touch. Carry them with you all the time."

"Got it." I secured the cuffs onto my weapons belt and tried not to get the heebies. "What else have you got for me?"

"What else would you need?"

I glanced around the room. "I don't know. What are those?" I pointed to what looked like a mace, only it didn't look like the traditional mace. It looked like hypodermic needles had replaced the spikes, and the chain that connected the fun pointy ball thing to the handle was thin, like a cheap link chain you bought at the costume jewelry store.

"It's called an *urticate*. It's for slowing down shifters should they lose control." Sawyer moved over to the weapon and carefully picked it up by the chain. "Each needle contains a strong dose of ketamine, which will bring down a shifter in just a few seconds."

"Is it heavy? Why is that chain so thin?"

"It might be thin, but it's strong. The elves made it."

I held my hands out in front of me. "Stop. Just stop. *Elves* are real?" What rock had I been fucking living under my entire life?

"Of course, they are. Who do you think makes all these things?"

"I don't know. And frankly, I don't want to know. Ignorance is bliss."

"You know what? When it comes to you, I believe that."

I shot him the finger, then pointed at what looked like a fishing net. "What does that thing do?"

"It holds merpeople without rubbing off any of their scales."

"And rubbing off the scales of merpeople is bad because…?"

"Because they die," Sawyer finished for me, using that same tone.

"Huh. Merpeople. Where do they all live? In the ocean?"

"Some. Some live in lakes."

"Swimming pools?"

"Only if you're unlucky and a water sprite has cursed you."

"What the fuck, dude? Seriously?" He couldn't have been telling me the truth there. It was too weird.

"Nah, there's no such thing as water sprites."

"No water sprites, but merpeople. Got it." I pretended to jot that information down into my invisible notebook. Remember that rug I told you about? The one that was no longer under my feet and a flaming remnant of all my beliefs? Yeah, that was all ash now.

Fuck me.

I felt so small.

Shaking myself, I asked, "Can I have a cool weapon? Please?"

"Cool?"

Man, that word sounded weird coming out of his mouth. It made him seem like he was a lot older than he looked. "Yeah, you know, something that can slice a man in two if I want it to."

He laughed, the sound deep and weak-knee-inducing sexy. "Why would I *give* you a weapon? You're dangerous enough on your own."

"See, here's the thing, I'm human," I said slowly. "H-U-M-A-N. I don't have super strength or invincibility. I'm fragile, and if I'm going to be going out in the field where other things are stronger than I am, I want something to protect myself with, since clearly, a standard-issue sidearm is *not* going to cut it."

He pursed his lips. "Perhaps I can find something for you." He perused the racks, stopping in front of a broad sword.

"Ah, I can't carry that," I told him, eyeing the weapon.

"I can assure you, you can." He picked it up. Damn, he made that look easy. "It adjusts to the strength of whoever wields it. So for me, since I'm strong, it's a little heavier, but still perfectly balanced for me to wield and be deadly." His gaze shifted to me. "But since you're a little shorter, a little weaker—"

"Hey! I object to the short comment."

He gave me a smug smile. "The truth hurts sometimes."

I flipped him off again. Twice in ten minutes? We were going to be best friends.

"In any case, the sword will adjust to whoever is holding it." Flipping it around, he cradled the blade in his hand carefully and presented me with the handle. Like he was a goddamn king or something. I snorted. What a douche.

Licking my lips, I took the handle in my hand and felt it settle into my palm like a cat cozying up to its owner. I braced my muscles for the weight, but even as I picked it up, I overcompensated and stumbled back a step. Holy shit. It was so light.

I turned the blade over in my hands, studying the steel…or at least, I thought it was steel. It could have been some funky composite material I'd never heard of before, which was probably accurate.

"Its name is Reaver."

"Why does it have a name?"

Sawyer leaned his hip against a small table off to one side.

"Names have power in our world."

"Oh?"

"For example, a fae will never give you their real name, because if you knew it, you would be able to exert a certain amount of power over them. Nobody likes being controlled."

"Is it just the fae that are strange with names?"

He shrugged. "Some vampires are too, but the fae are the ones who really take this no name matter to heart."

"Is Sawyer your real name?" I asked, flashing him a smile at the subtle frown he gave me.

"It's Sawyer to you."

Damn it. "Well, I'm just Cat. There's nothing special about me."

He shifted his gaze from my face to my chest. It was barely a flicker of movement, but it was enough to make the opal warm. I had no idea what was going on with the damn thing. It was just a necklace up until this morning. Now, it acted like it had a mind of its own.

"We shall see how special you are, just Cat."

Clearing my throat, I asked, "Can I keep this?" I raised the blade a little to show him what I was talking about.

"For now." He fingered the sharp edge of the blade delicately. "It seems to like you."

"How can a sword like someone?"

His crystal gray eyes met mine. "Magic doesn't play by the same rules that we do."

I loosened my grip on the hilt, the idea that the sword was real magic that was touching my skin, and that it actually *liked* me was next level. The opal flared briefly, then settled back into body temperature warmth.

"How am I supposed to carry this thing around. Do I need a permit?"

Sawyer actually laughed at that. "No." He tapped something at the base of the blade, a glyph I hadn't noticed, and the sword simply disappeared.

"Well, this is great and all." I motioned to my now empty hand, but it wasn't empty, was it? I could still feel the hilt lying snug against my palm. "It's still there."

"It is. It's simply vanished from view…for now."

"Ooo, sounds ominous."

He ignored my comment. Smart guy. He was learning quickly. "It'll reappear when you need it."

"How will it know?"

Again, he gave me that infuriating shrug. "Magic knows what the heart wants. Plus, if you blood the blade, it'll be more in tune with you."

"Look, I don't know a lot about magic and the supernatural world, but forgive me if I don't jump at the idea of *cutting* myself and *bleeding* all over the blade. Magic can be sinister and unforgiving."

"A lot like people," he said. "If you don't want to blood it, that's fine. It'll still work. Still kill. But it won't be as receptive to you."

"But you just said it liked me."

"It does. But liking someone does not bind you to them. Sharing blood will though."

"I think I'll pass."

"Suit yourself."

He gestured for my sidearm.

I was hesitant to give it to him. "You're not putting blanks in it, are you?"

"No. Silver ammunition. Silver can damage a lot of supes."

"Let me guess, you won't tell me which ones."

He shook his head, reloaded my gun, then handed it back to me. With the conversation clearly over, he turned around and began selecting a couple of blades and a gun that looked like it had come out of the old west. He strapped the blades to holsters on his thighs and concealed the gun in an underarm holster. I had to admit, if I saw him coming for me, I'd probably piss my pants...after I threw my panties at him.

"Ready?"

"Sure. But where are we going armed to the hilt as we are?"

"Elementary school."

I grunted. "It would have been cooler if you'd said 'hell.'"

"How do you know 'elementary school' isn't a euphemism for hell?"

I nodded. Well, he had me there.

4

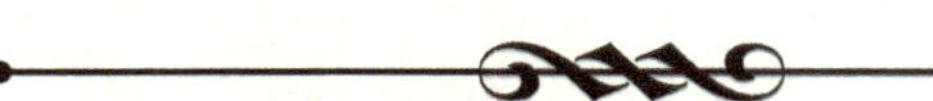

We didn't go to hell. We rolled up in front of Buxton Elementary School before pulling into the parking lot. We'd taken my truck because apparently, Sawyer only had a motorcycle, and there was no way in hell I was about to jump onto the back of that thing.

"Could you have driven any more slowly?" he asked, irritated, from the passenger seat.

"Possibly, if I'd known it would piss you off so much," I shot back sweetly. I'd always been a careful driver. Taking the driving test at the academy had stretched my limits of fear of dying in a fiery, fiery crash. I'd still passed, so I *could* drive like I was being chased by a dinosaur, but chose not to when I didn't have to.

"We could've been here twenty minutes ago if you hadn't balked at the idea of my bike."

"Seriously? You *seriously* expect me to get on the back of that death-trap with you when I hardly know you?"

"What does knowing me have to do with it?"

I put my truck into park. "If I don't trust you, I'm not getting onto the back of a freaking bike with you."

"You fill my heart with warmth," he replied in a drawl.

"Hey!" I shoved my finger into his chest. "I'm the snarky one in this relationship."

He growled. "Noted. Now get out of the truck because this is getting weird."

He had no idea what weird was. But I got out and waited for him at the tailgate. He prowled along the side of the truck, his face a mask I couldn't read. He was definitely playing bad cop today.

"You want me to do the talking in there?" I asked.

"No," he barked.

"Geez, you could at least let me down easy," I replied, secretly happy that I didn't have to take the lead. I would've been happy to just disappear into the background.

"Just keep your mouth shut and your ears and eyes open."

I mock saluted him. "Yes, boss."

He led the way into the main reception area and walked up to the desk. The older woman behind it looked up and smiled. She was dressed in a pressed-to-within-an-inch-of-its-life dress jacket that I suspected had a matching skirt hidden beneath the desk.

"Can I help you?"

"I'm Detective Taylor with PIG. We're here about the incident that occurred last night."

"Of course!" the woman practically shouted. Clearly, she was excited the cavalry was here. She stood up and revealed the matching skirt to her jacket.

"Ha!"

Sawyer glared at me, and I shrugged.

"If you could follow me please?" the receptionist said, bustling through a door to our right. I trailed behind Sawyer, peering through every open doorway as I went. We eventually came to a closed door at the end of the hallways, the words 'Principal Watts' written on the front. The woman knocked, then popped her head inside briefly before ushering us in.

I stepped into the room behind my partner and looked around. The walls were covered in framed artwork…kids' artwork. There must've been hundreds of them, covering every single square inch of the walls. Either Principal Watts had a few dozen kids and grandkids of his own, or he was lucky enough to be given artwork from the students.

"Good morning. Thank you for coming today. Although, we were expecting you half an hour ago?"

Sawyer glared at me over his shoulder. "I apologize, Principal Watts," he said so smoothly, even I felt sorry for driving as slowly as I had. "All I can do is blame car troubles this morning."

"No problem. Shall we get down to it? Please, have a seat."

Sawyer sat in one of the chairs in front of the desk, and I took the other. The sword, which I'd put on my hip, got snagged, and

I had to shuffle around to make sure it slid in between the arm and seat. If I kept getting caught on stuff, I was going to leave it in the truck next time. Why couldn't it have shrunk as well as gone invisible?

Sawyer glanced at me before he tapped open the recording app on his phone and placed it on the table. "Can you tell me what happened last night, Principal Watts?"

"Yes. We had our Thanksgiving concert last night. We had our kindergarten and first graders backstage waiting to go on, when a young girl, who doesn't attend this school, was seen approaching a couple of students. Apparently, the young girl had candy and was trying to lure the children away from the rest of the group, but one of our teachers appeared and chased the girl away."

"Who was the teacher?" Sawyer asked.

"Her name is Jasmine Wolfe. She teaches kindergarten here."

Wolfe? "Can we speak to her?" I asked.

"I assumed you'd want to speak to her first," Watts said to Sawyer, and he nodded. Wait, had he just *ignored* me? Sawyer tapped my arm and tilted his head to the side. He wanted me to listen.

"What else can you tell me about what happened?" he asked.

"The children finished the play and were sent home."

Sawyer asked, "Did anyone see the girl again?"

"No." Watts sighed. "Apparently, the young girl wasn't human. She was a vampire."

"And who verified that?"

"Ms. Wolfe. She's a werewolf."

I sat back in my chair and muttered, "I thought this was a human only school."

Without looking my way, Sawyer said to Watts, "Can we speak to Ms. Wolfe this morning?"

"Of course you can. After you've chatted with her, I'll bring the two children who had direct contact with the vampire to my office so we can talk in private. I've already secured verbal permission from their parents."

"That would be helpful. Thank you."

Principal Watts rose from his chair and showed us out of the room. We entered the school from a different door, and I tried not to cringe at the amount of noise coming from each of the classrooms. I wasn't saying I didn't like kids. I was just saying I didn't want to hear them, see them, or be near them.

Eventually, we stopped at a classroom that had cut out painted hands all over it and the name of the class on the glass panel. Watts knocked, then entered without waiting, greeting all the children warmly. He told them he would be teaching them for a little while as Ms. Wolfe had to speak to the nice detective outside. Clearly, he was referring to me.

I said as much to Sawyer, and he shrugged. "He kind of doesn't even know you're here."

"Thanks. I appreciate that so much." I hovered my palm over my chest. "Right here."

A woman stepped from the classroom Watts had disappeared into. She had a sweet face, blonde hair, and blue eyes. She was rocking the sexy teacher look in a black pencil skirt and pale blue blouse. "Hello," she said, her blue eyes warm. "Mr. Watts said you were here to ask me some questions?"

Sawyer bobbed his head. "Is there somewhere we can talk in private?"

Jasmine took us into an empty classroom that was littered with art supplies. Dried clay was stuck to the tables and smeared on the backs of chairs. She perched on the edge of one of those tables and folded her arms.

"What do you need to know?"

"Can you tell me what happened last night?" Sawyer asked, recording the conversation once more.

Her throat worked before she said, "Last night, I was backstage with the children so I could usher them on stage when it was their turn."

I walked around the perimeter of the room, looking at the pictures hanging on the yellow walls. "What time was that?"

She folded her arms, pushing up her cleavage that peeked out between the V in her blouse. "Around six-twenty, if I remember correctly. The concert started at six o'clock, and we were about a third of the way through the program."

"How many children were backstage with you?"

"Just kindergarten and first grade. That's why I paused when I saw the second grade kids there. They should've still been out in the audience. When I approached the pair to find out why they were backstage, that's when I smelled the vampire."

"What do vampires smell like?" I asked.

She wrinkled her nose. "Usually like dried skin and earth. And old blood." She shrugged. "I don't know how else to describe it."

"So, two second graders were there. Where was the vamp?"

"Standing a few feet away, hiding in the shadows."

"What did she say to the kids?"

"They told me afterwards that the girl had offered them candy, but they were scared of her so they didn't take it."

"Smart kids," I murmured.

Jasmine shrugged. "I think it was just instinct, honestly. Human survival instincts are pretty strong."

"What did the girl look like?" Sawyer asked.

"Maybe eight or nine. No older than ten, I would say. Blonde hair. Blue eyes. She was wearing a pair of pajamas with little unicorns on them."

Unicorns, huh? Maybe I had the same pair. "Shoes?" I asked.

"Slippers. Also unicorns."

"Niiiice."

My comment was met with a glare and a strange look. Right, not cool talking about my love of unicorns while on the case. "Wait. Are unicorns real?"

Jasmine laughed. "If they are, I haven't seen them."

"Are you related to Captain Vaile Wolfe at Buxton PD by any chance?"

She flushed and looked away. "He's my father, yes. He's your boss?"

Fuck! I knew it! I knew Wolfe was a fucking supernatural, and a werewolf no less. That explained so much. I wanted to punch my fist into the air, but I held myself back. Getting back to the conversation at hand, I jerked my head in Sawyer's direction. "He's my boss right now."

"Upgrade?"

"Easier on the eyes," I said without thinking. Then blushed. "Fuck. Sorry. That was…wrong. Your dad is very handsome, some might even say hot—"

"Stop talking, McKenzie," Sawyer told me bluntly.

"Shutting up," I replied softly, letting out a shaky breath. I looked down, waiting for the ground to open up beneath me.

"Did you see where the vampire went?"

"She took one look at me and vanished."

"Like, she just ran away, right?" I asked. "She didn't poof into thin air."

"Only the really old ones can do that," Sawyer said absently. "Most vampires just move *very* quickly."

I swallowed. I felt like I wanted to just disappear into a safety bubble and never step out. I was getting a crash course on the supernatural world, and I was totally going to fail the quiz at the end.

"Could you scent where she went?"

Jasmine flicked her fingertips over a pleat in her skirt. "I tracked her to a window that had been left ajar. I think she got out that way."

"I thought vampires couldn't come inside a building without an invitation."

"That only applies to homes," Sawyer replied, cutting off the recording. "Thank you, Jasmine. You've been a great help."

She bobbed her head, her blonde hair shining in the overhead light. "Anytime. If I think of anything else, or if you have any more questions, you know where to find me."

She returned to her classroom, and we waited for Watts to come back out to meet us.

"Are you ready to meet the other two children?" At our nod, he led us down a series of halls, finally stopping in front of a classroom. "If you could wait here, I'll go and collect the students and take you back to the office for the interview. I will have to be present for that also."

"Of course," Sawyer said.

When we were alone again, I asked, "Why is he ignoring me?"

He smirked. "Given your height, I thought you'd be used to it by now."

"Wow. You are such a shit."

He sighed. "It's the sword you're carrying. It's magic, and humans have no magic in them. Therefore, they can't see you or the sword, since you're touching it."

"But Jasmine could see me just fine."

He conceded that point with a nod. "True, but Jasmine is a werewolf. She's tied to magic in a different way. She could see you, but Watts and the receptionist couldn't because they're human."

"What if I'd taken the sword off?"

"Then you would've been visible to them."

"I don't know whether this is welcome information or not."

"It's neither good nor bad. It just is."

Who the fuck was he? Yoda? *Good or bad, neither is. Is, it just.* I folded my arms over my chest.

A few minutes later, Watts appeared again with two small kids trailing behind him. The girl and boy looked petrified as they took in Sawyer in all his growly beauty.

"This way," Watts announced in a tone that even had me jumping to attention. We followed him back into the office, then each of us found seats, Sawyer and I in the two chairs in front of the desk and the kids taking a seat on the low sofa up against the wall. Like criminals facing a firing squad.

Watts sat behind his desk.

"Trish and Jack, this is Detective Sawyer Taylor. He's here to ask you some questions about last night."

Trish huddled in on herself and shuffled closer to Jack. They looked similar, both with dark hair and eyes. Since I was essentially invisible right now, I sat back and let Sawyer take the lead.

"All right, Trish and Jack, I'm going to ask you some questions, and I'd like it if you could answer them as truthfully as you can. Is that okay?" He waited for both kids to nod before he pulled out his phone and hit the record button.

"Okay, Trish, let's start with you. Can you tell me what happened?"

The girl nodded and wiped a finger under her nose. "I don't remember a lot, actually." She glanced at Jack. "I remember being in my seat, and then I heard her calling me. I couldn't see her, so I stood up and walked to where I could hear her more clearly. I found her waiting backstage. She said she had some candy for me and my brother, but we could only have it if we went with her. I didn't want to go. I remember feeling that, but the next second, I was walking towards where she was hiding. Jack followed me because we always go everywhere together."

As the girl talked, I looked at Jack, who was staring at me dead in the eye. I blinked, wondering whether he could see me, and if he could, how was that possible. I raised one eyebrow at him, and he frowned.

"Jack pulled me away from her before she could take my hand. That's when Ms. Wolfe saw us and scared the girl away."

"Did you know the girl was a vampire?"

"No. She looked like a kid, just wearing pajamas, which I thought wasn't right, but then I thought maybe she was part of the show and she was just in costume."

"Have you seen this girl somewhere else?" Sawyer asked.

Trish shook her head. "No, it was the first time. Jack hasn't seen her before either."

Sawyer's cool gray stare settled on Jack for a moment, then darted away. Jack still had his own eyes on me. Watching. Waiting. Although, for what, I couldn't tell. Around my neck, the opal began to pulse with power and heat. I touched it briefly, drawing Sawyer's attention. I gave him a look, and he shook his head…

And that was when Jack attacked me.

5

I leaped from my seat, just in time to avoid the hit from the fifty-five-pound kid. Well, he was supposed to be fifty-five pounds, but the bastard was strong. Too strong.

He clutched at my shoulders, trying to bring his mouth to my throat. I shoved him off me, sending him sliding across the floor. Watts ran around the desk and pulled Trish with him, taking cover behind the mahogany monolith.

Sawyer growled, "Reaver," at me. It took me a moment to register the command.

"On a kid?"

"He's not a kid," he replied in a bored voice. He fell into a defensive stance, lowering his center of gravity and wielding both of his knives like a badass. "He's been possessed."

"Like by a demon?" I side stepped Jack as he launched himself at me once more, the sound of his little body slamming into the filing cabinet behind me making me flinch. Whirling, I reached down to my side and willed the sword into existence.

On the far side of the room, I heard Watts gasp, then sputter, "W-Where the hell did she come from?"

Jack launched another assault, this time wrapping his hand around my ponytail and yanking. He wrenched back my head, and I screamed as he ripped off a hank of my hair. It fluttered to the floor like teal feathers around my boots.

"You little bastard," I swore, aiming a blow at his head with the sword. No, I wasn't trying to kill the little shit—just knock him unconscious with the pommel. I didn't know how I knew to do that, only that my hand, and perhaps the sword itself, was guiding me. I was never accepting a magical blade ever again. This shit was unpredictable.

"I hate this sword!" I yelled at Sawyer. He slashed at Jack with his knives, one blade catching on the kid's shoulder. The scream that came from his throat was no sound a human could ever make.

"You shouldn't. It'll save your goddamn life."

"Fuck you!" I hurled the words at him without any feeling. I was just scared, and when I got scared, I got bitchy. Jack screeched and charged at me. Again. I wacked him in the arm with the flat of the blade, knocking him off course. He slammed into the chairs Sawyer and I had been sitting in, toppling them. The kid recovered in record time, leaping up to his feet and baring his human teeth at me.

"McKenzie!" Sawyer barked. "Do it. He won't stop until one of you is dead."

Well, I had no intention of getting killed by a kid today, but I also had no intention of *killing* a kid. Jack's shrill battle cry echoed around the room, and I blew a lock of hair from my face. Tightening my grip on Reaver, I held it by my side, ready to react, to actually go through with what Sawyer was frothing at the mouth for me to do.

When he was too close to change course, I held the sword out in front of me with both hands and shut my eyes. The sensation of steel meeting flesh was one I hadn't felt before, and I could safely say I never wanted to feel it again.

The resistance suddenly fell away, and I peeled one eye open to see Jack disintegrating on the floor of the principal's office.

"Oh shit," I mumbled. I turned to Sawyer, who was sheathing his knives.

"Touch the sword to his body, McKenzie. Finish it."

Biting my bottom lip, I lowered the tip of the blade to his arm. The flesh instantly turned black and began to flake. I blinked, unable to wrap my head around what I'd just done…and that's when I heard screaming. Trish was wailing over and over again, her eyes on what was left of her brother.

Watts had an arm protectively around her shoulders, and his free hand balled up against his mouth.

"Put the blade away." Sawyer crouched down beside what was left of Jack, running his fingers through the ashes. "Fascinating."

"It's not fascinating," I barked. "It's…it's…" I had no words.

What could I say anyway? I hadn't meant to kill a kid today, but he had attacked me first.

"What happened, Detective Taylor, and who is this woman who attacked my student?" Watts demanded angrily.

"He attacked me first," I shot back sullenly, glaring at the principal, who was only just seeing me now.

"He wasn't your student," Sawyer's words were calm and oozed authority. "He'd been possessed."

Watt's blanched. "Possessed? Possessed by what?"

"A vampire. He'd been made into a Renfield, a vampire's human slave."

"A slave?"

He nodded. "A vampire can feed off someone once and not create a slave, but multiple feedings achieve that." Sawyer turned to Trish. "Has your brother come home with any strange marks in the last few weeks?"

Trish swallowed. "He had two mosquito bites on his wrist last week," she said softly.

"They weren't mosquito bites."

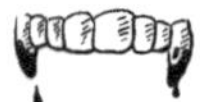

WHEN WE ARRIVED BACK AT THE STATION, I TOOK OFF REAVER AND handed it back to Sawyer.

"I don't want it," I said when he looked at me strangely.

"Don't be a fucking baby."

"It made me invisible!" And there was the real reason. I was short. Life was shit already. Add invisible to the mix, and I was downright savage.

"Yes, and if you hadn't had it, Jack would've killed you."

I snorted. "I think you're reaching a little there. I would've been fine. I take kickboxing classes."

"I know. I've seen you there, and I've got to say, not that impressive." He stalked back into the office, dropping Reaver onto my desk. I wasn't going to say I was sullen, but I was definitely not happy with it. Fine, he didn't want the sword back? I wasn't going to pick it up again either.

Using the end of a pencil, I nudged Reaver off my keyboard and sat down. "What are we doing now?"

Sawyer was furiously tapping away at his own keyboard, a sneer twisting his mouth. Wow. How was that even sexy?

"I'm writing a report to my boss about what happened."

I craned my neck. "Are you including how I picked the receptionist was wearing a matching skirt?" He turned to glare at me. "Hey, don't be mad you didn't call it first." I made my hand into a gun and blew at the imaginary smoke. "You have to be quick with me."

He returned to his work, and I got busy staring at the sword again. Leaning in, I brushed my finger over the glyph, trying to see if I was seeing this right. It had changed into what looked like an etching of my face, and the hairs on the back of my neck stood on end.

"What is it?" Sawyer asked, suddenly there.

"The glyph." My hand shook as I pointed at it. "It's changed."

He pursed his lips, but other than that, he didn't actually

look that bothered. Me? I was having a stage two freak out. He shrugged. "Magic."

Like that was a viable explanation for everything? Seriously!

"When can we put it back?"

"Why would you want to? It likes you. It protected you."

"It made me invisible."

"For a reason," he countered. "It was meant to be yours."

"And if I put it back?"

Again, that infuriating shrug that could've meant *you're fucked* or *let's see what happens and pray it's not bad*. "I suspect it will come back again."

I stared at Reaver forlornly. "Why couldn't I have picked a puppy instead?"

Sawyer rolled back over to his desk and began punching out the email. "Because puppies piss and shit everywhere. Swords don't."

"Yeah, they just make me invisible."

I didn't appreciate the smirk on his face.

With nothing left to do, I began turning around in my office chair, watching the world go by. With every revolution, I saw the faces of my new colleagues begin to blur and bleed into one another. I didn't even know what kind of supes I was working with. I slowed to a stop, then stood up.

"Where are you going?" my partner asked.

"I'm going to chat with my co-workers."

"Are you sure that's such a good idea?"

"Are you saying I'm not charming?"

After a second, he waved his hands in their direction. "By all means then, go and mingle," he said dryly.

With a nod, I walked over to the only other female in the office who wasn't BDSM lady and plonked myself on the edge of her desk. She looked up from what she was doing and smiled.

Fangs.

She had fangs!

"Sorry," she said, dimming her smile so that the delicate points disappeared. "I forget to act human when I'm in this office."

"Don't worry about it. I do that all the time." I cleared my throat. "I just thought I'd introduce myself since Sawyer whisked me out of here so quickly this morning."

"I know who you are," she replied in a smooth, sultry voice. Man, that was sexy, and I wasn't even into women. "Officer Cat McKenzie. Rookie. Watched your partner die on your first day on the job. The demon who took him is still at large. You've been off for a week, stewing I suppose. Now you're here with us as punishment. Whether that punishment is for us or you, I don't know."

"That about sums it up."

"And you're short."

"Ouch. Hit me where it hurts why don't you?"

She gave me her fangy smile again.

"What are you?"

She frowned. "A Gemini?"

"No, I mean, what kind of supe?"

"Oh! Have a guess."

I took her all in, from her lustrous black hair, to her naturally ruby red lips and green eyes. She was stunning, plus she had a banging body. What? I could check out and appreciate other women. "Not a vampire, because it's light out."

"One point to the human," she murmured, amused.

"You're gorgeous…"

"I appreciate that, but not interested."

I waved my hand though the air, batting the idea away. "Yeah, me either, but I can tell another woman she's hot and not get weird about it."

She smiled and nodded for me to continue.

"Not a shifter."

"What makes you say that?"

I jerked my head in the direction of the guy who had growled at me before. "Not growly," I said with a shrug.

She threw her head back and laughed. "I'm not possessive of office furniture. Nor do I growl unnecessarily. Do you give up?"

"Sure."

"My name is Faline, and I'm a succubus."

I practically leaped off the desk. "A succubus? Like you eat men?"

She snorted delicately. "I don't *eat* men. I drink from them."

"Ohhhh." I gestured to her mouth. "That's why you have fangs."

In a feat of creepiness, she stuck out her tongue—her nearly triple the length of a human tongue—and touch the narrowed tip to one of her fangs.

"They're just for fun," she replied, then cupped her hand up like she was telling me a secret. "They're like a tuning fork for orgasms."

"Wow. Overshare much?" I shot back, softening my snark with a smile. "Seriously, I want some. I'm all about the O."

"Are you now?" Leaning back in her chair, she smiled.

"So what is it that succubus do?"

"I feed on sexual energy. *Male* sexual energy, although in a pinch, a female's will do the trick too."

"Not as tasty?"

She snorted. "Not as potent. I get an almost euphoric high from male energy. I still get a hit from females, but it's about a tenth of that of men."

I glanced around her desk, looking for my next topic of conversation. "So, what is it you do here?"

"I'm just a detective, but I tend to take the sex crime cases. I'm pretty good at sniffing out the perpetrator."

"Figuratively?"

Faline grinned. "Literally. Lust is a scent to me." She eyed me appreciatively. "In fact, you smelled of it this morning."

"I did not!"

She turned back to her work. "Yep, you did. My nose doesn't lie."

When it was clear the conversation was over, I wandered back to my desk to find Sawyer watching me.

"What were you doing?"

"Just being friendly," I said with a shrug.

"Well, if you're done being friendly, we have to go and see a contact of mine."

"Who is it?"

"He. And his name is Alistair de Champ. He's a vampire in the local kiss who's agreed to see us."

I glanced at my watch. "It's one in the afternoon."

"Aware of the time," he said dryly. "Alistair is very old and doesn't sleep as long as the younger vampires."

Damnit, there was so much I didn't know. I filed that nugget of information away, then said, "Where are we meeting him?"

"His house. Don't forget Reaver." I glared at the weapon lying inert on my desk. "You'll want it," he added.

"All right, thanks for that ominous warning."

With a sardonic smile, he tipped an imaginary hat at me, and my middle finger twitched. I swiped the sword from my desk and willed it away.

6

Sawyer insisted on driving my truck this time, and I let him, only because I didn't know where I was going. Also, my hands were shaking so hard at the prospect of meeting a vampire that I probably would've crashed into a fiery ball of flames.

Mondays sucked.

"Why aren't there any squad cars for this department?"

"Supernaturals see red and blue flashing lights, and they're more likely to disappear. If we drive unmarked cars, we improve the odds of not scaring them away."

Well, that made sense. I guessed.

I counted to ten, then asked, "Tell me more about Alistair?"

He gave me a sidewise glance. "He's old and enjoys drinking from annoying human females with teal hair who run their mouths. Need to know anything more?"

I swallowed hard. "Nope. I'll just be over here repainting that target on my back."

He chuckled, and the sound was a shot of lust to my lady parts. Holy wow.

"Alistair has been my informant for a few years now."

"A few years? But supes have only been out for six months."

"True, but I was a PI for a decade before we all came out of the closet. I investigated cold cases that smelled of supernaturals."

"A *decade*? How are you any older than me?" He looked like he'd barely hit twenty-five.

"My species reaches maturity at around the age of twenty-three to twenty-five. After that, we stop aging, even though we gain years."

"Do I even *want to know* how old you are?"

"Probably not. It'll make you feel bad about yourself."

"Anyway, you're old, and we're going to see a contact of yours."

"Yes. He's a little different to most vampires. For one, he doesn't live with his kiss, although he is still a member of it."

"How does that work?"

"He's old enough to live alone. He can control himself, won't kill humans when he feeds—"

"Gross," I interjected.

"In return for his independence, Alistair pays a stipend to his mistress, Roxanne Monroe."

"Cool name. Does he know we're coming? Does he know *I'm* human?"

"Yes and yes. Don't worry. He has fantastic impulse control."

"I am all a flutter with confidence," I retorted bitterly.

After that, I shut up. I just watched as Sawyer smoothly drove my truck through to the most elite area of Buxton. Here, all the houses were set back from the curb. Elaborate gardens and fountains introduced the house before you got there, and as we made our way up the driveway, I balked at the gardeners working furiously in said gardens.

"Do they know who their boss is?" I jerked my chin in the direction of the slave labor force.

"I'm sure they have an inkling, although I've never asked them outright."

"They're not…*possessed* like little Jack Sullivan was?"

He flashed me a grin. "Nope. These people are just from a gardening service. As you can imagine, it's not like Alistair can come out and prune the roses himself."

"Lazy as fuck?"

I got a chuckle out of him this time. "Photosensitivity."

And another one of my life-long theories was put to bed.

He parked in the turning circle, and I got out of the truck, inhaling deeply. I didn't know what to expect. Maybe decay and death and bodies, but all I smelled was the crisp autumn air and freshly mowed grass. I looked at Reaver propped up in the foot well. It had slowly come back into view on the trip over here. I reached for it, then shook my head. I didn't need to make it some security blanket for myself. Mostly because it wasn't the soft and fuzzy cuddling variety. I shut the door and turned toward the house.

It was a gray marble monolith, a true tip-of-the-hat to British manor houses. A blocky 'C' shaped structure, there were long rectangular windows on both the upper and lower levels, each of them dressed in white gauzy material. Large topiaries filled the inside of the right-angled curve, all clipped and trimmed to within an inch of their lives. On the other side of the turning circle was a large fountain with Pan—the Greek God of the Wild—spewing water out of his pan flute.

The sun was warm on my face, and I took a moment to soak it in. While I was getting my shot of vitamin D, Sawyer knocked on the door. Having had my fill, I stood beside Sawyer under the large black wrought iron awning over the entrance way.

When the front door eventually opened, I yelped, but resisted the urge to dive behind Sawyer's legs and hide…

Because that would be unprofessional.

The impeccably dressed butler ran his eyes over me in disinterest. "Master Sawyer. How nice to see you."

"Hey, Charlie. Is his lordship around?"

What, like he was out back sunbathing?

"He's playing billiards in the games room. He's expecting you."

Sawyer stepped inside, and after taking one final deep breath, I followed him in. I tried not to gawk at the gold-veined marble under my boots or the expensive art hanging on the walls. There were also sculptures in their own niches along the walls, each with a little pot light above it. I was expecting a vampire to live in a crypt or something, not this light-filled palace and homage to art and culture.

The front door echoed as Charlie closed it behind us, and I peeked over my shoulder. He was watching me closely.

"He's a low-ranking fae," Sawyer murmured as we walked.

"And let me guess, Charlie is not his real name."

"Not even close."

"He works for Alistair?"

"I guess you could call it that. He's been with Alistair for as long as I remember."

"Companions then?"

He shrugged. "Sure. Let's run with that."

Sawyer navigated the house like he'd been there a million times before, and we soon arrived at a set of closed mahogany doors. He rapped his knuckles on one, then opened the door and stepped into the room.

"Sawyer." Alistair, I assumed, put down the cue he'd been lining up a shot with. "How are you?"

The two men shook hands, then Alistair turned his attention to me. "And who is this?"

"My new partner," Sawyer replied. I wondered how those words had tasted on his tongue.

"Ah. And to what do I owe the pleasure of a visit from you?"

Sawyer walked deeper into the room, running his fingertips along the red felt of the billiards table as he passed. "We have a case that I'm not sure about."

He wasn't sure about it? Then what hope did we all have? I stayed where I was, unwilling to get any closer to the vampire who was keeping one eye on me as well as giving his full attention to Sawyer. Honestly, I was impressed with the way he split his attention. He'd be a great work from home mom…you know, if work from home moms had fangs, drank blood, and were terrifying.

"What's it about?"

My partner blew out a breath and leaned against the side of the billiard table right beside Alistair, folding his arms over his chest. "Someone is turning children into vampires."

I studied the old fanger's face, but there was no shift in expression, not even a hint that he was shocked by Sawyer's declaration.

"I see," he replied dubiously. "Are you here because you think *I* made them?"

Sawyer shook his head. "No. I know you wouldn't be making children, but I wanted to know if you'd heard anything among your kiss?"

Alistair laughed. "I see our reputation as gossips precedes us." Wandering over to a bar in the corner, he opened up a small wine fridge and pulled out what I could've sworn was a blood bag from the hospital. He popped it into a microwave on the sideboard and hit a few buttons. The whir of the appliance was eerie, and I didn't think I could look at a microwave, let alone use one, again.

Blood in a bag. Gack.

The vampire became so still as he watched the glass plate rotate his meal that I wasn't sure he was breathing… Wait, did vamps even need to breathe anymore?

Both men seemed to wait, then, as if the *ding* from the microwave was the Pavlovian signal, Alistair came back to life and Sawyer let out a breath.

The vampire pulled open the microwave door, and my knees nearly buckled at the scent of warmed blood. "I have heard that there's a foreign vampire in town."

"And the mistress allowed this?"

With his baggy in hand, the vampire turned around and returned to the billiards table. Like it was a glass of expensive scotch. Not blood. In. A. Bag. I braced myself for the evisceration of that poor bag, but was stunned when Alistair pulled out a pair of small gold-plated cuticle scissors, snipped off one corner, and took a civilized sip.

"The mistress will allow most things if she can make a quick buck. She also allowed it to happen because this particular vampire was an acquaintance of hers from Italy back in the Dark Ages."

"Does this vampire have a name?" Sawyer pressed.

"It was never given, and I never press for such information. If it were important, she would've told us."

"Do you know where the guy is staying?"

Alistair shook his head, sending his still blond curls into rapture around his youthful face. "I'm not privy to that information, but I do know he wouldn't be staying with my mistress. Acquaintances for vampires," he said, staring at me, "are much like acquaintances for humans. The term means they aren't quite friendly, but they're known to each other."

Sawyer straightened and held out his hand to the vampire. "Thank you. I appreciate you talking to us."

"My pleasure," he replied smoothly, upending the bag and taking another delicate sip.

I tried not to make a face.

Sawyer led me from the room with his hand on the small of my back. I didn't want to admit how nice that actually felt, so I shrugged him off as soon as the billiards room door was shut behind us.

"That went well," I said cheerfully. "You know, except for the blood." I shivered. Sawyer's mouth was tight, but he didn't say anything more until we stepped from the house and got back into my truck.

"He knows something," Sawyer said, mostly to himself. "He didn't answer my question."

"He also said he didn't know," I pointed out helpfully.

"People can't lie to me." He tapped his nose. "I can smell it."

"First, ew. Second, seriously?"

He nodded. "Vampires, like the fae, are very good at telling half-truths or skirting around the truth, but Alistair was flat-out lying to us in there."

"What are you going to do?"

"There's nothing I can do. He knows we have an interest now. He'll tell his mistress, and I have no doubt we'll be going to visit her soon."

"I think I might be sick that day."

He raised one perfectly groomed dark brow at me. "Scared, pussy cat?"

"Don't call me that." My words were sharp, but not because of anger. Sawyer buckled himself in, then started the engine. It was close to five, which meant I only had an hour or so to get to my kickboxing class across town…if we were actually done for the day.

He drove us back to the station with an efficiency and economy I couldn't help but admire. I looked at his profile as we drove, wondering why I found him attractive at all. Sure, he had that chiseled jaw and knife-straight nose, but his mouth was always in a firm line, pressed hard and unyielding. My gaze drifted down to this crotch, where I wondered what else I might find that was hard and unyielding.

He looked over at me and frowned. "Are you having a seizure?"

I felt the heat rise to my face. "Over what? You? Being in your presence?"

"It wouldn't be the first time."

I snorted and brushed away some lint from my pants. "You have a really high opinion of yourself."

"I have high standards, and those high standards guide me and my decisions."

I rolled my eyes and said, "Please don't tell me you're into the power of mindset."

"And what if I was? Some of the most successful people are fanatical about mindset. Ever wonder why?"

"No," I shot back, suddenly curious to know more. He was

impassioned about this. "But why don't you tell me, guru?"

He ignored both the comment and me until we were bumping back into the stations' lot and parking between two other cars.

"What do we do now?" I asked, getting out.

Sawyer glanced at his watch. "It's nearly six. We'll start again fresh tomorrow, I think."

I held out my hands for the keys to my truck, wiggling my fingers. He threw them over the top of the cab, and I caught them after a small fumble. He smirked.

Douche canoe.

Back inside the station, I stashed the sword back into the arms room, then grabbed my bag from under my desk. As I walked to the door, Faline stopped me.

"Got a hot date?" she asked with a sweet smile.

"Kind of? I've got a kickboxing class."

Her lusty, lusty eyes lit up. "Ooo, I love kickboxing. Well, have fun!"

I gave her a wave, then walked back outside and got into my truck. I took a quick detour home to get changed, then made it to the gym just in time.

7

"Cutting it fine!" Mike called from his position in the center of the mats where he ran the warmup drill.

"Sorry!" I dumped my sports bag on the side, toed off my shoes and joined the circle of people running. Sasha sidled up beside me, barely breaking a sweat.

"Working late?"

"Had to see a man about a vampire," I shot back.

Sasha's brows rose, but she said nothing more.

I got lost in the warm-up, feeling my stressed body ease as the endorphin rush hit it like a freight train. As soon as we broke off to do some kicking drills on the weight bags, I found Sasha once more and pulled her to the one farthest away. Sliding behind the bag to hold it, I motioned for her to start on the kicks. Mike was being a dick today, making us do one hundred fast kicks on one leg before swapping with our partner. I enjoyed the moment of peace while Sasha slammed her shin into the bag and sent it rocking ever so slightly. Damn, the girl was strong.

"Did you really go see a vampire today?"

"Yup." I repositioned my hands, so she didn't accidently kick me.

"I thought only PIG handled cases like that."

Oh, shit. I hadn't told Sash what had happened. Feeling like a terrible friend, I gave her the CliffsNotes and smugly enjoyed the way her eyes bulged.

"You're working with PIG? But you're not a supe."

"Noted," I conceded with a nod. "But my boss thought it would be funny for me to work with them."

She finished her last kick and came back into a neutral stance, lowering her arms. Sasha didn't sweat, she glowed…and she was glowing her ass all over the place tonight. "Swap," she breathed.

Being careful not to walk in the way of someone else's stray kicks, I found my position and, at Sasha's nod, I began, calling out my number as I went.

"So, the case you're working…?" Sash asked.

I shook my head, cursing when I landed a bad kick that got more of the top of my foot than it did shin. "Can't talk about it."

"Less talking and more technique," Mike shouted, right over my shoulder, then walked away.

I glanced at Sasha, who only smiled. I got my hundred kicks out on my right leg, at which point we swapped again and made our other leg feel like Jell-O. Switching off my brain at kickboxing was one of the things I loved. I just got lost in the technique and instruction. Being on the mat didn't require me to be defensive, or to even think about my past. I just got to live in the moment, in the sweat and the comradery of being surrounded by other people who liked it too.

When the class finished, I hugged Sasha and told her I'd call her about dinner on Friday night. We usually got something to eat and then hit the bars afterwards. She needed to blow off steam regularly, given she was a high school teacher and had to put up with emotional teenagers' shit all day.

I waved goodbye to her, then retrieved my bag from the sidelines. I collapsed beside it and pulled off my wraps and shoved them inside. Next, I took off my ankle guards and gave them the same treatment. A few people milled around after class, casting appreciative looks over near reception. I looked too, because I'm nosy, and stiffened at the sight of Faline standing there.

She was wearing a pair of leggings that did absolutely nothing to hide her banging body, and a tight tank top which highlighted her fantastic breasts. Seriously, why couldn't I pull that off?

I glanced back at the guys from my class who were still casting furtive looks her way. Those poor bastards. They wouldn't know what hit them.

"You should go and talk to her," I said as I passed. "She's single." I had no idea whether that was true or not. If it was, I just did her a favor.

"Cat!" Faline called, motioning me over.

I shifted the strap of my bag on my shoulder and made my way to her. "Hey."

"I didn't know this was where you took your class."

"This gym is the best," I said, narrowing my eyes at her. "How come I've never seen you in here before?"

"I usually do the nine o'clock class, but since I got out early tonight, I decided on the earlier one."

"Who teaches this one?" Because Mike sure as shit didn't.

"His name is Skeen. He's some sort of elemental."

"Elemental?"

The succubus touched me lightly on the shoulder and laughed. "I keep forgetting you still don't know a lot about us. He's a fae who can control the elements, but he specializes in fire."

"Good to know," I replied. I would not freak out. I would not freak out.

She looked over my shoulder and smiled, and holy shit, that smile was mesmerizing. I peered over at what she was looking at.

"Friends of yours?" she asked.

"Classmates, I guess." I watched her for a little longer. "Are you feeding off them?"   My question snapped her gaze back to mine, and she grimaced, then shrugged. "Maybe a little? I find aggression and sexual energy to be tightly entwined, so hitting up gyms like this gives me a nice little pick me up."

"How often do you have to feed?"

"A few times a day."

"What if you can't find food?"

She laughed lightly, although I could hear the strain. "There's always food around."

"What if you were stuck in a lesbian convention all day that had a strict no-dick policy?"

That comment got a more genuine laugh, and I much preferred it to that fake shit she was laying on before. "You know what? I like you, Cat McKenzie."

I didn't say it, but I liked her too. I didn't want to, though. She was one of the monsters I feared so much. They weren't supposed to be likeable, or even approachable.

"*How* do you feed?" My question caught her off guard. "Sorry. You don't have to answer that."

She waved away my concern, then turned when a guy appeared and started barking orders at them all. She shrugged and moved in the direction of the mats, dropping her bag and bouncing lightly on the balls of her feet. I leaned against one of the support beams and watched how the lithe muscles in her legs helped her move with a grace that was almost feline. She wasn't too thin, like most women were these days. Instead, she had sculpted muscles in her arms and shoulders, like she used to be a dancer or something.

The warm-up began, and where us mere mortals had had to run around in a circle, here they took running leaps that covered the entire mat, or defied gravity itself and ran directly up the walls in a wide arc.

The longer I watched, the more the opal against my heart heated up. With a sigh, I waved goodbye to Mike, then drove home, stopping for pizza at the joint only a block from my apartment.

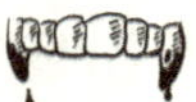

I woke with a gasp in the middle of the night. Out of instinct, I reached for the opal, then thought that was stupid. The thing wasn't a weapon. Honestly, I didn't even know why it did what it did.

I jerked at the sound of a fist hammering away at my apartment door, then I cursed whoever it was for waking me up at two in the freaking morning. Didn't they know I needed my beauty sleep? Tossing back the comforter, I stuck my feet into my unicorn slippers—*no*, they aren't *just* for five-year-old girls—and slipped on the matching robe.

Whoever had woken me up was still hammering, and at this rate, the whole floor was going to be privy to the screaming I was about to rain down on the sucker.

"What?" I hissed as I yanked open the door.

Sawyer pushed past me and into my apartment without so much as a hello. He was still dressed in the black slacks and black button-down he'd worn to work that day…err, yesterday. Had he even gone home?

"What are you doing here?" I asked, shutting the door. "And please, do come in."

He threw me an acerbic look.

"Not a morning person. Noted." Shuffling into the kitchen, I got the Krups going and leaned back against the counter. "What are you doing here?"

"You didn't answer your phone."

"Umm, yeah, because I was asleep."

He shook his head. "Crime doesn't care what time it is."

I actually laughed out loud. "Oh my god, how many nineties cop show re-runs have you been watching? Seriously? *Crime doesn't care what time it is*," I mimicked, pulling open an overhead cupboard and pulling out a mug. Sawyer didn't get a cup of coffee this morning. Grouchy people deserved none.

"Why didn't you answer your phone?"

"It didn't ring." I didn't mean to sound defensive, and I sure as hell didn't mean to sound petulant, but Sawyer had a way of bringing out the immature side of me. "The battery must have died."

His hands curved into fists at his side, and he sucked in a deep breath. "Unbelievable."

I arched a brow but continued making my coffee. If he thought he could come into my apartment at two in the morning and berate me, he was living in a fucking alternate universe.

While I finished making my coffee, he stalked around my living room. "What's with the unicorns?" he asked, amusement coloring his voice, just like his blood was going to color my walls if he didn't stop making fun of my unicorn collection.

"I like ceramic unicorns."

"They're a little childish, aren't they?"

"You're a little childish," I shot back. Definitely not my best retort, but it was early. Waaaaaay early. Plus, I hadn't had any caffeine. "What are you doing here? Not to chat. I suck at small talk."

"I know," he replied, lowering himself on my couch. He stretched his arm over the back of the cushions and waited. "I got a phone call thirty minutes ago about a body down by the docks. The human department is down there right now preserving the crime scene."

"Why not us?"

His mouth softened. "Because our department is a team of five and a CSI we do not make. Plus, it's not within our responsibilities to do that."

I poured myself a cup of coffee, then begrudgingly offered it to Sawyer.

"No, thank you. But we need to hurry. Every minute we waste erodes scent trails."

I chugged my coffee, immediately regretting the decision to go without creamer, and placed it into the sink. I had a feeling I wasn't going to be getting any more of that sweet, sweet caffeine jolt anytime soon.

"Give me five," I told him, rushing back into my room to get changed. Since Sawyer was in his finest cat-burglar outfit, I decided to forego my uniform and slipped into a pair of black skinny jeans and a black cable-knit sweater. Just as I was sliding my feet into my motorcycle boots, he knocked on the door.

"Just a sec. I need to do my hair."

"Dead girls don't care about your hair," he called back.

"Well they should," I mumbled under my breath and stood up.

Despite Sawyer's bitching, I pulled my hair up into a messy bun, then met him outside. He gave me an appreciative look, and I could swear his eyes darkened for a split second.

"Ready?" he asked.

"Sure. Do you want to take my truck?"

"If you don't want to freeze your ass off on the back of my bike, then yes, I think we should."

Scooping up my keys, I looped my badge over my head and put on the gun holster, checking the safety was on and I wasn't going to accidently shoot myself in the foot. I lead the way down to the street where my truck's windshield was getting icy. I approached the driver's side but stopped when Sawyer cleared his throat imperiously.

I glared at him. "It's my truck."

"You don't know where you're going."

"You could tell me," I retorted.

"This will be faster," he replied.

Grumbling, I threw him the keys and walked over to the passenger side. "You're a control freak."

His laughter was sharp in the early morning air, slicing it in two. "Oh, if only you knew."

Sullen and cold, I got in and pulled the seatbelt across my body. Sawyer coaxed my truck to life an instant later, no early morning coughs or jerks like normal. Resting my elbow on the door, I leaned my face into my palm and watched the still resting Buxton fly past the window. I didn't bother asking him any questions about where we were going and what I should expect to find. I'd been living in this town all my life, skirting the edges of the part of town known as Hell.

It wasn't that we were poor. My parents had bought a large apartment building due for dereliction downtown back in the late nineties. They'd spent a solid year renovating the whole thing, then began letting out apartments to friends of theirs. They were both archaeologists, but after I was born, my mom stayed at home more and more.

Until, on her first dig in nearly eleven years, she went missing.

I assumed she'd been killed, but murder was a hard concept to swallow for a nine-year-old. From then on, it was just me and my dad. He didn't cut back on work. If anything, he worked even more, and I was left in the care of a neighbor called Mrs. Brown. She would spend more time at our place than she would in her own, and became the woman I went to when I got my period at thirteen and then when I had my heart broken by Chris Pachinko in high school.

"Cat?"

I shook my head and turned to Sawyer. "What?"

He studied me for a moment before returning his attention to the road. "I just asked if you were sleeping."

"No, just…thinking."

He raised an eyebrow at that statement but didn't look at me again. Only five minutes later, we entered the docks. Sawyer drove us to a section that was labyrinthine, the giant steel containers stacked into rows which seemed to twist around when I was expecting linear order. I was suddenly glad he did drive.

Like hell I was going to tell him that though.

I got out and shivered. In my haste to get out of the apartment, I'd forgotten to grab a jacket.

"Here," he said, throwing something at me. It was a navy-blue jacket that had the letters PIG written in yellow on the back. I slid into it, zipped it up, and followed Sawyer down to where yellow tape cordoned off the crime scene. I ducked under the tape behind Sawyer and stood back while he spoke to the responding officers.

Two large four thousand watt tower lights had been set up to illuminate the scene. Laid out in front of me was hundreds upon hundreds of shipping containers, each ranging from green to red to white and every other shade in between. Some were stacked at least seven stories high. The light that was being cast by the tower lights didn't reach much beyond fifty feet though, leaving a clear demarcation of artificial day and shadowy night.

"Come on," my partner told me, urging me toward a set of three shipping containers stacked one on top of another. The middle one had its doors thrown open, and I tilted my head up to see if I could see anything other than darkness.

"It's up there? How in the hell did they find the body?"

"Anonymous tip," he replied, scaling the side of the container like it was piece of kids' playground equipment. When he got to the top, he motioned for me to follow. "Come on."

"Um, I'm not part monkey, so I can't climb up there."

I expected him to fight me on it, but he simply shrugged and took out his phone, turning on the flashlight function. "Stay right there then. I'll take photos so you can study the scene."

I mock saluted him and watched him disappear. About thirty feet away, the rest of the cops milled around, not straying farther than the reach of the spotlight. I looked the other way, into the darkness not twenty feet away, and shivered as a wicked breeze blew past me.

Beneath my sweater and jacket, my necklace began to pulse with heat. Narrowing my eyes, I scanned the shadows around me.

"Can we get any more light down here?" I called out to one of the responding cops. I thought his name was Smith.

He shook his head. "There's something funky going on. We can't get any closer than this. We tried to set up a light right where you're standing now, but it wouldn't turn on." He jerked his chin in the direction of where the light was now. "This is as close as we got where it would work. There's some sort of magic in use here. That's why we called you freaks in."

His colleagues laughed at the jibe. The fucker was lucky I was standing where I was and too lazy to walk my ass back up there. Grinding my teeth, I looked at the shadows, then to where Sawyer's flashlight was bouncing around inside the container. Another sharp gust of wind winged past me, the surrounding containers forming a tunnel. It seemed to call to me, that wind, and I took a step forward, straining my eyes to see who was there.

Because someone *was* there.

With one more furtive glance in Sawyer's direction, I took a couple of steps into the darkness. I'd maybe only gone about fifteen feet when there was an audible *pop* and something brushed against my cheeks and neck. I tried not to twitch, because it felt a lot like spiders running over my skin.

I heard my name again, but this time, I heard it more clearly. Like whoever was there was only just past the next stack of containers. I reached for my side arm and held it down by my thigh. My skin still prickled like hands were running over it, stroking me and urging me farther into the dark.

"Hello?" I called, wincing when my voice echoed like I was standing inside a large room instead of the open air. Acoustics aside, the containers would have absorbed the sound rather than bounced it.

The opal burned a little hotter, and I moved it onto the outside of my jacket. The pale blue light it gave off allowed me to see a little more clearly. Now that I was in this sludge of darkness, the moonlight was a little better, although when I looked up in to the dark, starless sky, I couldn't see the moon. That was tip-off number two that shit was not going well.

Sliding along the edge of one container, I kept sweeping the area with my gaze, looking for whatever the hell was going to jump out and make me pee my pants.

"It's Buxton PD. If you know anything about the crime that's been committed here, you can come forward."

I stiffened when laughter bubbled out of the darkness and the opal glowed more brightly. I was torn between wanting to find out who was there and getting the fuck out of Dodge, because something wasn't right here. I spun around, intending to leave, when I jerked back a step.

There was a woman standing before me. An old woman, and not as in a woman who had been weathered by time. This woman looked as if she'd been aged in the sun, her skin thick, black, and leathery. Her eyes were milky white and opaque, so I figured she was blind. But if she was, where did she come from, and why was she out here in the middle of the night… or was it early morning? I guessed it depended on how you looked at it.

"Hello?" I took another step back. The woman smiled, her jaw unhinging like a snake's to reveal row after row of razor-sharp teeth. My necklace started to glow even more brightly, and I slid my foot back another step, shuffling away. The old crone watched me, tracking my movements like a hungry wolf, although I was sure her eyesight was gone.

"Ma'am?" I asked, swallowing. Gagging. Gagging on the smell of dead things and old blood.

The woman lifted her claw-like hand, complete with fingers double the length of a humans and tipped with inch-long curved blades for nails, and reached for me. I lifted my gun and took aim, squeezing off a round that ricocheted into one of the steel containers behind us and pinged into non-existence.

I'd shot her in the chest, but it had had no effect. It'd simply gone straight through her chest cavity and exited out of her spine. I took aim again, this time putting three into her—two in the chest and one in the head.

"What are you?" I asked, even though it was stupid. What was she going to do? Stop and tell me?

She hissed through her sharp teeth and came at me again. I danced backwards, trying to come up with a plausible explanation for this. I knew crazy shit happened to me, but this was taking it to the next level. I emptied my clip into the woman and swore when she screamed like a banshee and threw herself at me.

Ducking off to the side, I watched her fly past me, slam into the container, and crumple to the ground. Now I was torn. There was a woman who looked like she was ninety-five years old, in the cold, wearing nothing but a thin nighty, yet the other half of me—some might say the intelligent part—wanted to kill the bitch with anything at my disposal.

I staggered backwards, then screamed when something strong closed around my arm. I spun to look at my attacker and actually breathed out a sigh of relief.

"Oh, thank God, Sawyer."

His eyes narrowed on the crumpled heap behind me. "Stay here," he said, then strode towards the bundle of cheap frills. Crouching down, he pushed the old woman's hair from her face, then leapt back onto his feet. And about four feet away. At the same time. Really, it was quite a feat.

"What is it?" I asked, huddling into my borrowed jacket. It was warm, and the smell of sandalwood and something else deeply masculine tickled my nose.

"Not what," my partner said, returning to my side but keeping his eyes glued to the old woman. "Who."

"Who?"

"Baba Yaga."

"Baba…" My voice trailed off with my thoughts as I tried to recall who that was. I knew the name. I snapped my fingers. "The *witch* from fairy tales?"

Sawyer's expression was grim as he nodded. "The body of that child had been partially devoured."

"Can you give a girl a little warning before you say stuff like that?" I told him hotly, resting a hand to my stomach. I was starting to feel a little queasy. That may have had something to do with the *goddamn nightmare* from children's stories attacking me though.

He glanced back over at Baba Yaga, like he was waiting for her…or the Antichrist to rise. Hell, maybe they were the same thing.

"Is she dead?"

He shook his head. "Just stunned."

My laughter, which I'd tried to contain, came out as a snort. "Yeah, that's because she brained herself of the corner of a shipping container."

"She isn't known for her intelligence." He looked down at my gun and frowned. "Those bullets should've stopped her though."

"They didn't." I shrugged.

He studied me for a minute, then said, "Let's go. I've collected as much evidence from the scene as I can."

As we walked, Sawyer stayed close, his hand protectively on the small of my back, but the sensation of spiders crawling all over me came back, and I shivered. I felt Sawyer stare at me but chose not to look. Yup, I was brave like that. My ears were suddenly equalizing, and we stepped back into the pool of light. The cops were still there, but now there was an ambulance and the coroner too.

It all looked the same, except for the faintly lightening sky. It would be dawn soon. I glanced at my watch and was horrified to discover it was nearly four-thirty. I'd been with Baba Yaga for over an hour? How was that possible? It only felt like ten minutes had passed.

Sawyer said something to the cops standing by the tape, then guided me back to my truck. With each step, it felt like my body gained twenty pounds, weighing me down and sending a wave of lethargy over me. I couldn't wait to crawl back into my bed again.

"You need to eat," he said, opening up the passenger door and gesturing for me to get in.

"I need to sleep more."

"Food first." He slammed the door, then jogged around to the driver's side. I snuggled down into the jacket and shut my eyes. Maybe I could get five minutes while we drove to wherever the hell we were going.

8

“Cat?” Sawyer murmured, his warm breath feathering over my skin.

“I don’t want to go to school today, Dad,” I said, squeezing my eyes more tightly.

He heaved a sigh, just like my dad would’ve done. “We’re here. I’m not carrying you in there.”

I peeled open one eye and looked at him. Fuck, he was hot. I frowned. “You could bring food to me out here. It would save you time, because I’m pretty comfortable right here.”

“Jesus,” he muttered under his breath, running a hand through his hair. His sexy hair. *Fuck!* What was wrong with me? I was suddenly all hot and heavy for teacher? Although, if I was being honest, I was secretly already crushing on him.

“Okay, okay,” I said reluctantly. I had to change the subject, otherwise my brain was liable to make me jump his bones and then things would be awkward at work. I slid from the car and would've collapsed onto the asphalt, if it weren't for Sawyer's arm on my elbow.

"Easy, pussy cat." His words were soft, careful…caring maybe. "We're just going to walk over to the door, then you can collapse all on your own again."

Reaching up, I pinched his cheek. "Such a sweet talker."

He jerked his head away with a snarl, and I smiled, leaning heavily on him. I felt like the energy was draining out of my feet, and all I wanted to do was sleep.

"Cat! Wake up!" Sawyer shouted. His grip on my arm tightened, and I realized I actually *had* fallen asleep on him. What the actual fuck was going on? I concentrated on getting through the door of the twenty-four-hour diner he'd brought us to, slumping down into the booth when we got there. Instead of taking the seat opposite, Sawyer sat beside me.

"Don't get handsy," I slurred, resting my head on the table.

"I'm just making sure you don't list sideways and fall on the floor. You'd be a trip hazard."

"Mmmm," I said, already drifting off again.

I jerked upright when Sawyer pinched my thigh under the table, and I frowned at him.

"What the fuck was that for?"

"You need to stay awake."

"I am awake," I replied indignantly.

"No, you're drooling all over the table like it's made of candy."

"Try Channing Tatum." Unfolding my arms, I placed them on the table and forced myself to sit upright. It was a struggle, because it felt like someone was literally sucking all the energy from me.

"The food will be here in a minute." Sawyer's soft murmur gave me some sort of peace, and I nodded.

"Food…"

He listened, rapt, like the next thing I was about to say would be gold. "Yes?"

"I like food."

He snorted softly. "I already know this."

Lifting my hand in front of me, I see-sawed it from side to side. "Why do I feel like I've been drugged?"

He pursed his lips. His gorgeous, sensual lips.

I blinked, then shuffled over a little.

"You, pitiful human," he began, smiling, "waltzed into Wonderland tonight."

I blinked again. It was like I'd just learned how to do it and wanted to practice it every freaking second. *Wonderland?* I'd gone into Wonderland? How was that even possible? How was I not dead right now?

"I resent that word."

"Human?"

I growled. "Pitiful."

"Ah, the food," he announced, thanking the old-looking waitress with a nod. He shuffled the plate of pancakes over to me, dousing them in syrup. I grimaced.

"You need sugar." Next came a plate of liver. Seriously, what kind of diner was this? "And you need iron."

I shoved the liver away, my face scrunched up. "I'll eat pancakes. Not liver. It is *not* war time and it is *not* 1950."

He gave me an exasperated sigh but nodded. "All right. You eat it all up like a good girl."

"I hate you." Picking up the knife and fork, I cut into the short stack angrily and stabbed a piece while picturing Sawyer's face. Putting it into my mouth, I moaned a little at the taste. He was right, the bastard. I was hungry and I did need food. Sawyer sat back and watched me with a smug expression on his face, like the cat that got the cream. He sipped his coffee, never taking his eyes off me, until I placed the last slice of pancake into my mouth and swallowed. At this point, his eyes had taken on a predatory gleam I wasn't sure I liked so much.

Pushing the plate gently across the table away from me, I lunged for the coffee cup and drank greedily. I felt possessed, like I wasn't in control of my own body.

"It's the aftereffects of Wonderland," Sawyer said, narrowing his eyes on my face. "Humans aren't supposed to be able to enter."

Okaaaay, I didn't like the way he was now looking at me like I was a science experiment. Twisting my body around, I placed my back against the wall of the diner and stretched my legs out.

Grinning, I said, "What can I say? I'm a special cupcake."

If there was one thing I had going for me, it was bravado. I was used to acting—pretending I was taller, pretending I was stronger. I'd been doing it my whole life. The one thing I didn't have to pretend was being human. Because I fucking was.

He shook his head and took another sip of coffee. "You are most definitely human, but what you did tonight…" He drifted off, clearly caught in the snare of his own mind, yet he didn't take his eyes from me.

I finished the dregs of my coffee and nudged him with my foot. From the expression on his face, he was affronted that I'd touched him with my boot. Still, he slid from the booth with that preternatural grace all supes seemed to have—well, except for giants. Those fucks were as uncoordinated as new baby giraffes, or so I'd heard.

"And where are you going?"

"Bathroom." I arched a brow. "Unless you think I need an escort? Are you volunteering for the job?"

He made a disgusted sound in the back of his throat. "By all means, go and use the bathroom. We'll be leaving as soon as you get back."

I gave him a salute, sauntering through the small diner that used to be an old dining car and down the short hallway that housed the single male and female bathrooms. After relieving myself, I took extra time scrubbing my hands, trying to get the stickiness of the syrup off. It felt like I'd just shoveled the food into my mouth with my hands.

When I stepped out of the bathroom, I only managed three steps before I stopped. It happened just as the door to the diner opened and shut, letting in a crisp breeze. The opal around my neck began to heat up with steady warmth. Wrapping my palm around it, I took a cautious step out of the hallway and into the diner proper. Sawyer was still seated at the booth, head bent over his phone. Everyone else was just eating or chatting. Even the waitress hadn't noticed the small girl who had wandered in.

Her clothes were torn and dirty. She had no shoes on her feet, and her long, dark hair was matted and stringy, falling over her face and shielding her eyes...

Eyes which were trained on me. I could feel them like a second skin.

Or like daggers aimed at my heart.

To test my awesome theory, I sidestepped to the left, and the little girl mirrored me. I stepped to the other side. She followed. I stepped back, and she advanced. I kept my arms loose by my side but let my gaze find Sawyer, who was *finally* paying attention to what was going on. He frowned, looked at the girl, and then turned back to me.

Kill her, he mouthed.

WTF? He wanted me to kill the elementary school kid? I couldn't do that. I was still getting flashbacks from when I'd run that other kid through with Reaver in the principal's office. If I had to commit filicide again, I was going to get a complex.

Plus, how was I supposed to commit said murder? The clip in my gun was empty, thanks to Baba Yaga, and Reaver wasn't even here. Man, I wished I had that sword though. It felt so good against my palm, so right. It was an extension of my arm, even though I'd never picked up, let alone used a sword before. Guns had always been my preference. I suddenly felt something in my palm, and when I looked down, I saw Reaver there.

My eyes widened and then darted to Sawyer. His expression was unreadable, but he nodded to me like he knew what I had to do. I lunged for the kid, who didn't actually move like a kid. She was *fast*. She leaped above my head and landed behind me. I swung around to face her once more, just in time to see her throw herself at me. She crashed into me with more strength than should've been possible and took me down. Reaver was knocked from my hand, and I watched helplessly as it skidded across the linoleum tiles.

I turned my attention back to the kid-slash-fucking-freak-of-nature and yelped when she smiled at me with dainty little fangs peeking out from her top lip. She was a vampire? It was an assumption, given that Faline also had fangs, but come on! What were the chances that she *wasn't* a vampire?

"Sawyer," I called desperately, shoving my forearm against her throat and pushing, hoping to dislodge her. On anyone else, the move would've cut off the windpipe and air supply. It was too bad for me vamps didn't breathe.

She snapped her teeth at me, her fetid, dead-for-a-couple-of-days breath feathering over me. I shoved her back again, barely gaining an inch. As we grappled for advantage on the floor, I heard Sawyer herding everyone out of the diner, making sure no humans got caught in the crossfire. What was it about me that made me a vampire magnet?

My arm began to shake as my muscles, still weak from my

jaunt into Wonderland, began to fail.

"Sawyer," I breathed. "I can't hold her much longer."

A heart beat later, the weight of the small child was lifted from me, and I blinked at Sawyer standing above me, his front to the back of the baby vamp, his arm wrapped around her throat, holding her. The bitch was still struggling to break free. A strange hissing sound escaped the vamp's infant throat, and I shivered at how wrong that was.

"Are you okay?" he asked, his voice strained with the effort.

Standing up, I brushed myself off and stared at the vampire, being careful not to look in her eyes. They could control someone like that, right?

"Where did she come from?"

He shook his head. "I don't know, but we need to get some answers. We'll take her back to PD and put her in the holding cell—*Fuck*!"

I was suddenly on my back again, the vamp on top of me with her mouth open over my throat. It had been barely a second, then Sawyer was there, heaving her off me.

"Do you have those cuffs?" he asked as he wrestled the girl back into a standing position. I breathed heavily through my mouth, then slapped a hand to the sting on the side of my neck. It came back red.

"She bit me," I told Sawyer indignantly. I glared at the girl-vampire-whatever. "Bad vampire!"

"You'll live," he barked back. "Open the diner door. We'll cuff her at the car."

With a slight tremor in my hand, I picked up my sword, which shouldn't have been here, then did as Sawyer asked and opened the door, following him out into the pre-dawn.

"We only have maybe thirty minutes to get her back to the station before she poofs into ash."

"You're cleaning my backseat if we don't make it in time," I grumbled, touching my ravaged throat again. I glanced around then and saw all the staff and customers of the diner standing in the parking lot, staring at us with wide eyes.

I held out my badge and said, "Buxton PIG. Go about your business."

I wasn't sure whether they would listen to me, since I looked like an extra from *The Walking Dead*, but I was relieved to see them all walk away. Jogging to catch up to my partner, I opened up the rear door of my truck for him first, then dropped Reaver onto the passenger seat. Snagging the cuffs from the center console, I snapped them onto the vamp's wrists. She immediately stopped snarling and hissing. Sawyer eased her onto the back seat, where she sat calmly and stared ahead.

"I like these cuffs," I told Sawyer. He grunted and shut the door.

"Are you all right?"

I touched my neck. "How bad does it look?"

"Let me see." He slid his fingers onto either side of my jaw, tipping my head this way and that. "You'll live. It'll be sore for a while though."

I shrugged. "Pain. My old friend."

He looked up at the sky. "We need to go."

I let him drive on account of the stiffness already setting in to the muscles around my neck and shoulders. Vampire bites were a bitch. I took the twenty-minute drive to replay the whole fight, as well as the whole fucking night. How my sword had appeared in my hand with a thought, I didn't know.

"How did the sword come to me? I locked it back into the arms room when I left last night."

He glanced over at me, the instruments casting a soft glow across his sharp cheekbones, but the darkness hid the other half of his features. "It's magic. And like I said, it likes you."

I stroked the steel. "Are you telling me it's sentient? It has thoughts and feelings?"

He shook his head, flipping on the directional signal like he was driving at noon rather than six a.m. "Sentient isn't the right word."

"Well, what is the right word? If I have a magical object following me around, I want to know the details of why."

He shrugged and said helpfully, "It's magic. Magic doesn't play to the rules of the world as we know it. It has its own. All I know is to respect the hell out of it because if you don't, it'll screw you over."

"So, it just *likes* me?"

His mouth flexed into a soft smile. "Something like that."

I stroked the hilt again. Well, as far as friends went, having a bloodthirsty blade at my disposal wasn't so bad. "Will it ever leave me?"

"If it does, it won't be something you can change. Magic is like the wind. It's in flux, and it's more mercurial than most women I know."

"You're hanging out with the wrong women," I muttered.

"And how would you know—"

Sawyer's words were cut off suddenly as we went from driving in a straight line to flipping through the air. I tried to keep count of the revolutions, but it was like being on a demon rollercoaster and the brakes were broken. The windshield buckled and shattered with each revolution, eventually shattering on the third spin. Glass sliced my face and neck, but it was all a drop in the ocean compared to the pain in my shoulder. I think I screamed…

Then it all went to black.

9

Intermittent light flickered somewhere close to my face as I regained consciousness. It only took a second for the pain to make itself known, forcing me to suck in a low moan that would've sounded porny and hot if it weren't for the blood… or the broken glass. In front of me, all I could see was asphalt. Tiny flecks of glass congealed in my own blood sat in puddles around me. I shifted my eyes over to the right when I heard a shuffle. Sawyer was there, stirring slightly.

Opening my mouth to talk, I found my voice suddenly gone. I swallowed and tried again. "Sawyer? Are you okay?"

"Hmmm?" He had a thin coat of dust on him, covering the shoulders of his shirt.

"Sawyer?" I hissed. I didn't know how long either of us had been unconscious for, but the sky outside had already gone from the cool gray of dawn to a bright orangey-pink. The sun had risen. I couldn't hear any sirens yet, but they would come.

I hoped they'd come.

My partner was still hitting the ZZZs, and honestly, I would've been right there with him if it wasn't for the need to get the fuck out of here. The pain in my shoulder was a dull throb, the sensation content to sit in the background for now. I knew when I moved, all that would change.

Craning my neck, I tried to figure out how we had landed. The car was on its side, with me at the bottom and Sawyer hovering above me, only staying put because of his seatbelt. The windshield was gone. All the windows had been shattered, and the smell of gasoline hung heavy and noxious in the air.

I was all for waiting for the cavalry to arrive, except there was a small wisp of black smoke curling up from under the hood. The tendril weaved and dance with the air current. Heat would follow if that spark got enough oxygen to it.

We had to get out of here by ourselves.

Inching my hand around, I slid it down to where the seatbelt clipped into the socket and pressed the button. Nothing happened, even after I jiggled the damn thing and cursed at it for good measure. Sweeping my gaze around the car, I glanced up at Sawyer dangling above me, and spotted the still sheathed dagger on his thigh. Straining, I reached up to grab it and was thankful my fucked-up shoulder was on the other side.

Sliding the knife free, I wrapped my palm around the hilt and started cutting the nylon strap holding me in place. It came apart easily under the knife, which was pretty convenient. I also noticed I didn't have to saw at the thing. The blade just cut through it like it was…well, a knife through butter. I'd have to remember to ask him about that later.

Once I was free, I dropped the knife and called again to Sawyer.

His eyes flew open as he inhaled sharply. They were wild as he looked around, trying to process the scene. He stared at me, blinking.

"Hey, it's okay," I told him. "We need to get out of here though. I think it's going to catch fire any moment now. Can you undo your seatbelt?"

He nodded, and I braced myself because he was hovering a few feet above me in the air, and once the belt was gone, there was only one way to go. I tried to shift away as much as I could, but he landed awkwardly, showering us both with dust.

I coughed, hissing out sharply as the movement jostled my right shoulder.

"You're hurt?" he asked suddenly.

"I also can't breathe on account of you sitting on my chest right now."

"Fuck. Sorry." He shifted a little, letting me suck in a breath of dusty, smoky air.

"Can you crawl through the windshield…well, what's left of it anyway?"

He looked at the space and nodded. "Yes. I'll slide out, then come back for you."

"Great plan," I wheezed out, my vision alternating between

sharp clarity and eighties Vaseline-rubbed camera lens. "Go do that."

Sliding from the wreckage, he almost looked graceful, and I wondered whether I could do the same thing. Probably not. A few seconds later, he was gone, and my chest tightened a little. Rationally, I knew he was just outside the car, but as far as my pain-addled brain was concerned, he'd abandoned me at my hour of need.

"Sawyer?" I called hoarsely.

"I'm here," he said. "There's an ambulance on the way."

"Can you get me out?"

My eyes were trained on the opening he'd disappeared through, but I jolted back when his face popped back into view.

I sucked in a pained breath.

"Sorry, he said. "I need to at least try to get you out before—Fuck!"

Alarmed, I demanded, "What? What's happened?"

But he didn't have to answer. The black smoke that had just been a tendril before was now billowing thickly. The cloud rose quickly from the car, along with the heat of an intense fire.

"Get me out of here, Sawyer." I wasn't above begging if that's what he wanted.

He disappeared, and I sucked in a sob. He was going to leave me here because I was a sucky partner and nobody wanted to work with me. This was karma wrapped up in a flaming car wreck. There was a sound, like something metallic tapping. I looked down and found my sword waiting patiently for me.

Shifting my uninjured arm around my body, I picked it up from the footwell and stared at it.

"Can you get me out of this?" I asked it.

"Cat, we need to find the sword."

"It found me," I called, relieved he hadn't abandoned me.

"You can't come through the front like I did. The flames are getting more intense. Can you use it to cut open the roof? I think I can pull you out that way."

Looking up, I studied the roof. It had been peeled open like a can at some point, just not over the front section of the truck. Lifting up the sword, I swore as my shoulder pinched. Shoving that pain aside, which was *hard*, FYI, I focused on the sword.

"Can you open the roof?" I asked Reaver softly. "Can you get us out of here?"

The sword began to glow with a pale blue light, and I touched the tip to the half-shredded roof. The sound of heat-buckled steel filled my little bubble of pain, and I watched as the metal literally melted where the sword touched it. I was starting to sweat now, as the heat from the fire in the hood intensified.

The sword stopped glowing, and then there was a Cat-sized hole in roof.

"Thank you," I told Reaver, then more loudly, I shouted, "I've made a hole."

Sawyer appeared in said hole, his eyes widening as he saw what a good job Reaver had done. Reaching inside, he grasped my good arm and started to pull. I bit my lip as each move sent daggers of pain through me. I think I may have passed out, because when I came back to, I was out of the car, lying on the cold asphalt thirty feet from my destroyed truck.

"There you are," he said with a small smile. "You passed out from the pain."

He was looking down at me as he cradled me in his lap. I tried not to think about how weird that was. And by weird, I meant I couldn't wait to get my head in his lap again. You know, once my shoulder stopped throbbing.

"Noted," I replied, my fingers curling involuntarily around the hilt of Reaver.

"You've got a big bump on your head. The EMTs want to take you to the hospital."

That was when the world dumped awareness on me. I flinched as flashing lights and the sound of sirens and people shouting hit my senses like a sledgehammer

"How's our patient?" someone asked above my head. I shifted my gaze to the EMT standing there. He was tall, muscled, and smiled like he genuinely cared. "Awake, I see."

"What did I miss?" I rasped.

He crouched down beside me. "Oh you know, the explosion. The firemen with their hose."

"I hope they were naked." I shut my eyes. "But they kept it classy with bow ties and strategically placed Santa hats."

The EMT laughed. "The drugs are working just fine, but that bump on the head is a concern. We're going to take you to Buxton General."

"But I don't have a reservation," I whined, earning me another good-natured chuckle.

"She's a hoot," he said, obviously to Sawyer.

I felt my partner brush his fingertips across my forehead. "She's something all right."

"They're just bringing the gurney over now. She'll be in safe hands with us."

I shut them out at that point. They were talking about me like I wasn't even there. I didn't owe them my consciousness.

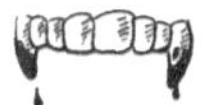

When I woke up, I was in hospital, wearing a thin gown and tucked into a bed with over-starched, too-thin sheets and blankets. I sucked in a deep breath through my nose and let it out through my mouth. Well, at least my nose wasn't broken.

The door to my room opened, and Sawyer walked in. He was in clean clothes, his hair slightly damp from the shower he must've taken. The bastard. I was still covered in soot from the accident and subsequent fire.

"You're awake," he murmured, placing down the cup of coffee he'd gotten from a vending machine, if the cup and smell were anything to go by.

"Live and in color."

"How do you feel?"

I tried to shuffle up in the bed, wincing when a dull throb in my shoulder told me to stay the fuck still. "Like I got hit by a semi?"

Sawyer shook his head ruefully. "You're not far off it. We *were* hit by a semi."

"Ha," I replied dully. "I hope you got his insurance details." His smile was warm, and I tried not to think about how that made my lady-parts feel. "What happened?"

Shaking his head, he took a seat on the side of my bed. "Someone ran us off the road. Whoever they were, they wanted us dead."

I let that sink in. I was used to being disliked. With a mouth like mine, not many people *did* like me, but I'd never had anyone wanting to commit murder.

"What happened to the vamp?"

"Ashed. In the rising sun."

"Damn it. She was our only lead."

Sawyer shook his head. "She wasn't worth losing your life over."

I grunted and placed my hands down at my side… where I felt Reaver. Sawyer, seeing my expression, also looked.

"How did you convince the nurse to let Reaver in the room?"

"I didn't." He laughed and shrugged. "Magic?"

Heaving a sigh, I held back all my questions. This sword had a freaking mind of its own… Although, if I was being honest, I really liked its mind. It had saved my life on more than one occasion.

"When can I get out of here?"

"Well, the doc said your shoulder was only dislocated. He popped it back into the socket, but you'll have to wear it in a sling for a day or two, and it'll still be sore for a couple of weeks."

"That's why they invented drugs, right?"

"Right."

"You also have a few deeper cuts on your hands and some shallow ones on your face and neck from the shattered windshield. Add that nasty bump on your head, and you're all set to strap in for a drug-induced haze."

He grinned.

I whimpered.

Reaching out, he tucked some of my hair behind my ear and exhaled. "Other than that, they think you're okay."

"Does that mean I can go?"

He shook his head. "As soon as you have something to eat and can keep it down, you can go."

"Great. Let's do it. I hate hospitals."

10

After I proved I could keep a sandwich down, I was discharged from the hospital with my right arm in a complex sling, a fresh set of scrubs to wear home and more pain drugs and instructions than I could keep straight in my head. Reaver had conveniently disappeared without me touching the glyph at all whenever a nurse or doctor came in, and now I had no idea where it was. A cab was waiting for us, and after Sawyer helped me in, I expected him to shut the door and send me on my way.

That didn't happen.

He jogged around the back of the car and got in the other side.

"What are you doing?" Okay, that sounded accusatory, and I hadn't meant it that way. I guessed I was just shocked.

"I'm making sure you get home safe."

I glanced around. "Are you being filmed? Did someone pay you for this? Am I being Punk'd?"

He frowned. "Why would anyone pay me for this? You're my partner."

I let his words settle into my psyche. Partner. He wanted me as his partner. Or at least for right now. Maybe the next time I fucked up, he'd jump ship.

"Okay." I cleared my throat. "How are you? It looked like you didn't get injured at all in the crash."

He tugged the neck of his shirt down, revealing a sculptured chest I wanted to lick chocolate off of. He smirked, then pulled it down a little further, revealing a thick red welt across his chest.

"The doc said it'll be bruised for about two weeks, but I should be fine."

"Seriously? That's all that happened to you? I get a dislocated shoulder, and you get a *bruise*? Is that because you're a supe?"

"No, it's because the truck hit us on your side." He eyed me curiously. "By all accounts, you should be dead. I don't even know how the side of your truck wasn't a ball of twisted steel… well, *more* of a ball of twisted steel."

"Maybe we got lucky?" I absently ran my fingers over Reaver's hilt, which was lying across my lap. That was strange. It had disappeared as soon as the orderly had come in with my sandwich, and I didn't bother to look for it. Somehow, it had just turned up in the taxi. I wasn't going to think about it too much.

"Maybe," he murmured. "I've been meaning to ask you…"

"Yes?"

"Your necklace, the stone. It's opal?"

I wrapped my fingers around it protectively. "Yes."

"Where did you get it from, if you don't mind me asking."

I stiffened at his words but shook myself. Sawyer wasn't the enemy here. "My father gave it to me after my mother died. He said it was for protection."

"I'm sorry about your mom."

I shrugged, even though thinking about her still made my heart hurt. "It happened a long time ago."

"What about your dad? Is he still around?"

"No." The word was hollow, and it sounded hollow coming from my lips. "He was murdered about five years ago."

"Shit. Sorry."

"What for? You didn't kill him."

"I don't mean that," he said. "I mean, I'm sorry you've lost both of your parents. It's tough being out in the world by yourself."

"After my mom passed, my dad kind of threw himself into his work with an almost fanatical fervor. I wouldn't see him for weeks, sometimes months on end. When he did come home, it was only to collect some information before he was off again."

"What did he do for work?"

"I don't know exactly. They were both archaeologists, so I assumed he was on digs."

"Who looked after you then? You couldn't have been old enough to look after yourself."

"I wasn't. Our next-door neighbor, Mrs. Brown, looked after

me. She spent more time at my place than she did her own. She ended up moving in for a while, right after my mom died, because my dad just disappeared one night and didn't come home the next day. In the end, he was gone for about six months, so I was lucky to have her."

Reaching out, Sawyer stroked his thumb over my knee. "I'm sorry."

Shaking myself, I said with a cocky lilt, "We're all a little fucked up, aren't we?"

I looked out the window to see we were turning onto my street. When the cab stopped, Sawyer paid him, then helped me upstairs to my apartment. He tried to take me to my bedroom, but I shook my head.

"Shower first. I've got vampire in my hair."

He smirked. "I bet you've never said that before."

I grunted and shuffled toward the bathroom. Sawyer followed at my back like a shadow, pushing things out of the way when needed and holding my elbow when I swayed.

"I'm okay," I said. "Just a little nauseous."

"The doc did say you might feel like that. It's all part and parcel of the side effects from the painkillers you're taking."

"I never want to be hit by a semi again," I grumbled, then turned on the shower. I was about to undress, but stopped when I couldn't get the sling off my right arm.

"Do you mind?" I asked him.

Sawyer approached me, slowly releasing the three clasps that held the sling against my side. I concentrated on his strong fingers as he worked the straps free then gently eased my arm out. When I sucked in a hiss of pain, his eyes shot to me.

"Did I hurt you?"

I shook my head. "I'll be fine." Hooking the thumb of my free hand into the waistband of the scrub bottoms I'd been sent home in, I tried to pull them down and soon realized this was not a solo endeavor.

"Will you let me help you?" I eyed Sawyer warily. "You won't be able to do this by yourself," he pointed out. "Plus, I've seen plenty of women naked before. You don't have to be shy on my account."

"I'm not worried about your sensibilities," I grumbled in reply. But he was right, of course. I couldn't do this on my own. With the ache in my shoulder and the pain in my knee, I was a fall hazard waiting to happen on a wet tiled floor.

"Look, the doctor said I needed to keep an eye on you tonight so I can either help you or you can go without a shower, which I don't think you want to do."

I didn't have the energy to argue with him. All I wanted was to get the vampire off my skin and out of my hair. "Fine."

With a nod, he crouched down and slid the thin fabric from my hips. I didn't have any underwear to take off since the doctors had removed every stitch of clothing when I was rushed to the hospital. Keeping my eyes fixed on the tiled wall in front of me, I cooperated when Sawyer told me to bend a knee or keep myself steady by leaning on his shoulder.

"Okay," he finally said in a hoarse voice.

Slowly, so as to not fall over and have Sawyer crow his victory over me, I stepped into the shower and promptly listed to one side.

I braced for impact, but Sawyer was there, holding me up with an arm around my back. I huffed, then peered over my shoulder to find his silver eyes hot and liquid.

"You're still dressed," I said, although why that was my first concern, I didn't know.

"My clothes will dry." He shuffled me closer to the spray, where I turned my face into the water and hissed when the small cuts on my skin let their presence be known. Adding more cold water to the mix, I tried again, sighing when all I got was a slight throb. Putting my face under the flow fully, I let all the ickiness from my day sluice off me.

"Want me to wash your hair for you?" he asked, his breath warm against the shell of my ear.

I nodded. Honestly, he could've offered to cut my toenails and I would've said yes.

Leaning me gently against the wall, he grabbed my shampoo and squeezed a little into his hand. I shut my eyes when he ran his fingers through my hair, creating a lather.

"Head back," he said, and I did as I was told, for once, and shut my eyes as tepid water cleaned away the suds. I thought that was it, but he rubbed some conditioner through my hair too, letting it sit while he washed me.

I leaned with my back to the wall, watching my fully clothed partner rub my coconut-scented bodywash all over my body. He kept his hips angled away from me, but I could see that he was turned on by this.

"You don't have to hide that," I told him as he rinsed the cloth off.

"Hide what?" Water ran down his face, slicking back his hair. His shirt was sticking to his skin, clinging to the curves of his chest.

"Your erection."

He snorted but didn't say anything more.

"You don't think I'm attractive?"

He jerked his head up, his eyes gobbling up all the light in the room. At least it seemed that way. They went from gray to stormy tempest in a heartbeat. "Why would you say that?"

Shrugging my good shoulder, because talking about this stuff was just a smidge embarrassing, I tried to put my bravado back on… and discovered I may have left it at the hospital.

Rescuing me from the inevitable crash and burn, he said, "Let's get out of the shower."

Sawyer wrapped me in a fluffy towel and shoved me out the door. Glancing back over my shoulder, I watched him strip off his shirt, slacks, and underwear, leaving them in a wet pile on the tile.

"Enjoying the view?" he asked without looking my way as he reached for another towel.

Would it kill me to say yes? I shuffled to my room then I paused when I realized I couldn't put my favorite pajamas on without help. I turned to ask him for one more favor only to find him already there with a towel around his waist. Putting clothes on me felt more intimate than the undressing for some reason, so like an adult, I didn't look him in the eye as he pulled up the flannelette pants and did up the buttons on the matching shirt.

Without saying a word, he helped put the sling back on too.

"I'm going to throw my clothes into the dryer. Where are your clean sheets?" At my raised brows, he added, "I'm sleeping on your couch tonight."

"Bottom shelf of the linen cupboard in the hall."

I walked around aimlessly while he got busy making a bed for himself, trying to figure out what to do. I felt like I should be playing host even though I was clearly in too much pain to do anything other than lie flat on my back and stare at the backside of my eyelids.

"You should go to bed. I can entertain myself while you pass out."

Fantastic idea.

With a nod, I stumbled into my bedroom, shut the door, and laid down. My eyes were closed before my head even hit the pillow.

11

I woke the next morning to the smell of fresh coffee and pastries. I sat up, blinking blearily at the sun streaming through the windows. Out in the kitchen, I heard someone moving around. Throwing the blankets from my body, I padded out to find Faline. She took one look at me and said brightly, "Good morning, sunshine."

"What are you doing in my apartment?"

"Sawyer asked me to stop in on my way to work to make sure you were okay. He had to leave early this morning. I brought breakfast." She gestured to the plate of delicious, buttery pastries and the coffee. Still cautious, I sat down at the counter and reached for a plain croissant.

"Did Sawyer really send you? And how in the hell did you get in here without the key?"

She smiled, flashing me a little fang. "I asked your building manager."

"You mean you seduced my building manager."

She shrugged, all *who me?* "I may have had breakfast there too."

I held my hand up, the one brandishing the croissant, and said, "Argh. No. Don't tell me all the details."

Leaning her hip against the counter, she grabbed a pastry for herself. "So how are you feeling?"

I looked down at the sling. "Better than I was yesterday. I guess you've heard what happened then?"

She nodded, her silky black hair shifting off her shoulders. "I did. I'm sorry about your truck."

"Yeah, me too." I loved that truck. Shoving the rest of the croissant into my mouth, I swallowed a couple of mouthfuls of coffee and stood up. "We should probably get to work, huh?"

"The boss said we could come in at nine."

"That's only forty minutes away."

"I guess you'd better start getting ready then."

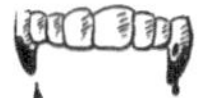

I SHOWERED IN RECORD TIME, HOLDING BACK THE YELPS AS THE water stung my cuts once more. Half an hour later, I rolled back through to the kitchen, finally dressed in a pair of black slacks and black blouse. It had taken me twenty minutes to get into them, but I did it, damnit.

Take that, Sawyer.

I found Faline was curled up on my couch, flipping through a year-old shooting magazine.

"I missed this issue," she said absently, not taking her eyes off the page. She looked up at me. "There's a great article on cutting and crowning a barrel with hand tools in here."

I nodded. "If only I had a workshop of my own," I said wistfully. "Are you ready?"

Standing up in one smooth movement, she eyed my clothes. "No uniform today?"

"I already stand out as a human in our department. Why draw any more focus?"

She smiled and made a smug little noise under her breath.

"What?"

"You said *our* department."

Shit. "Slip of the tongue."

"Or the truth? You like it with us."

I snorted and folded my good arm over my chest. "Yup, you got me. I love getting attacked by vampires, totaling my truck, and traipsing into Wonderland by accident." I hope she caught my sarcasm, because my words were dripping in that shit.

"Don't forget Reaver, who seems to have really taken a liking to you."

"Ah, yes, can't forget the sentient sword who's made it its mission to pop up at the most random times." I looked around and found it on the kitchen counter. Stalking over to it, I slid it into my belt loop. Damn, I needed to get something better to carry it in.

Faline studied me. "They always say less is more."

I grimaced. "I might as well take him back to the station this morning. No doubt he'll pop up again later anyway."

"True enough. Are you ready?"

Grabbing my badge, I drew it over my head, then looked for my side arm.

"Sawyer told me to tell you he has it. When you got to the hospital, they stripped the weapons off both of you, and he collected them afterwards."

"Good to know. Are you ready?"

She nodded, and we walked down the stairs together, our footsteps in sync. I sighed. I wished it was the nineties band.

"How's the neck feeling?"

"My…" I placed my palm against the bite there and winced. "Still sore."

"A baby vamp gnawed on your neck, but it should heal pretty quickly."

"You're sure? I don't want people getting the wrong idea about me and Sawyer."

She snorted, and even that sounded sexy. Bitch. "Sawyer wouldn't ravage your neck and leave you bleeding."

I raised a brow and pushed open the front door of my apartment building. "Oh?"

Faline gestured to a hot pink Fiat 500. "No. He'd also make you come. He's considerate like that."

If I'd been drinking coffee, I would've spat it out. As it was, all I could do was gape. She gave me a coy smile. "What? You are attracted to him, right?"

"Only in a platonic way." I was hedging and doing it badly.

She unlocked her car, and I slid into the soft cream leather seat. "Well, these don't come as standard," I commented, looking around the cream-on-cream interior.

"I like what I like," she replied with a flick of her hair.

"You know what? For a succubus, you are not what I expected."

"What did you expect?"

"Leather, whips, and chains."

She laughed, and it was a beautiful sound. "Oh, that's what my spanking room is for."

"You have a…spanking room?" I swallowed. Now, why did I like the sound of that? "Do tell."

Faline pulled out into traffic easily, sliding into the flow without so much as a horn blaring at her. "Some men enjoy being spanked. Some women do too."

"I thought you said you could only feed on male energy."

"That's right, but I just happen to like sex with women too. I don't feed off them. Sex with them is just my guilty pleasure."

"You sound like you're breaking all the rules."

She shrugged. "Not really. I'm old—"

I gave her a look, since it seemed like she was barely twenty-five.

"I *look* a lot younger than I am."

Flicking a hair from my slacks, I asked, "So how old are you?"

"I was born just before the breakout of the first World War."

I gaped at her. "Hot damn, woman." I shook my head. "Okay,

how old is Sawyer?"

"If I remember correctly, he was born in the sixties."

"Flower child. Got it."

She grinned. "No, not the nineteen sixties. The *eighteen* sixties."

Shock rippled through me then I cleared my throat and asked the question I'd been wanting to know the answer to for ages. "Have you two ever…?"

She looked horrified. "Had sex?"

"Well, yeah. I mean, you're hot. He's hot. You could feed off him, right?" Faline still had that deer in headlights look on her face, and I rushed to add, "Forget I mentioned it."

"I kind of can't now," she replied, then sighed. "As much as I would totally love for him to fuck me into oblivion, I wouldn't let him."

"Got a boyfriend?"

"No. Argh, could you imagine how hard it would be to feed if I had a boyfriend?"

"I thought it would've been easier?"

"We can feed from one source, but that's like asking you to only have one meal for the rest of your life."

"Ah, yum, mac and cheese me, please."

She shook her head. "What if every time you ate that mac and cheese, you lost nutrients and it began to taste like cardboard?"

"To be honest, I'm not sure box mac and cheese has too many nutrients to start with."

Laughing, Faline added, "Touché, but that's what it's like for me if I feed from one male exclusively."

"So even if you loved the guy and didn't want to go anywhere else…?"

"I would have to. Or I would die."

"Shit."

She fiddled with the radio, finding a station that was playing soft rock. "But if Sawyer and I were to screw, it would end with a pregnancy."

"He's got strong swimmers, huh? Wait, how do you know that?"

She gave me a strange look. "You do know he's an incubus, right?"

I literally felt the blood drain from my face.

"Shit, you didn't," she muttered. "I think he wanted to tell you himself. I just thought he had already."

"It's okay. It's not like we're getting married or serving a life sentence together."

"No, you just have to work with him and trust him at your back, and, Cat, you can totally trust him at your back. He's a good guy."

"An incubus? Really?" *Play it cool, McKenzie.* "So why is he a no-bang zone for you? He'll knock you up just like that?" I snapped my fingers.

"Whenever there's a coupling between an incubus and succubus, there's a child produced."

"I'm pretty sure that's why condoms were invented."

She shook her head. "The only reason a succubus and incubus would bang would be to reproduce."

"Well, if that wasn't an ad for abstinence, I don't know what is." I laughed, or at least tried to, but betrayal was a dirty, rusty knife being twisted into my gut.

"I'm sorry."

"It's not your fault. I knew I was working with supes. I thought I could handle that. I'm okay with you being a succubus. Why shouldn't I be okay with Sawyer being an incubus?" I laughed again, the sound edged with mania. "It wasn't as if I thought he was human."

I glanced out the windshield and was relieved to see we'd arrived at the station.

"Because he's your partner and you have to trust him."

"I do trust him," I replied automatically, frowning when I thought about the words. I did trust him. He came running into Wonderland for me. He saved me from the baby vamp. He pulled me out of a goddamn car wreck that should've left me a traffic collision statistic. I flushed when I thought about what happened when he took me home, took care of me.

"You're thinking about having sex with Sawyer right now," Faline said, gently, guiding her car into a free spot.

"Am not." I totally was. "How sensitive is your sex-o-meter?"

That comment got me a small, fang-filled smile. "Pretty fucking accurate."

"You can tell I'm attracted to him."

She touched me on the shoulder. "FYI, he already knows. Plus, he's attracted to you too."

I shrugged that last comment away. "But how much of that

is instinct to feed?" I replied. "I don't want to be an instinctual impulse." She opened her mouth to reply, but I waved her away. "What does it matter anyway? He's my partner. Partners don't fuck each other's brains out." Even though the thought of Sawyer leaving me sated and boneless was an instant shot of lust to my groin. Unclipping my seat belt, I got out of the car.

"I'm sorry if I've upset you."

Upset me? Popped my biggest illusion bubble? "It's not your fault. What he is shouldn't matter." I looked up at the building. "We should probably get in there though. We're already late."

12

I walked into the office behind Faline, listening to the sound of office chatter taper off suddenly.

"There she is, our own miracle child." This came from a guy called Braxton, who was sitting behind his desk with a grin on his face. He was a shifter of some kind, but I wasn't sure what yet.

"Miracle child?"

He nodded. "Congrats on being inducted into PIG."

I rocked back on my heels. "How do you figure?"

Holding out his hand, he checked off his fingers as he said, "Attacked by a Renfield, fought Baba Yaga, got bitten by a vampire, survived a run in with a semi, Reaver likes you…"

"Okay, okay," I told him. "I get it. I'm a bad-luck magnet."

He still had that stupid grin on his face. "Oh no, sweetheart.

You aren't just a magnet. You're the epicenter, and you're just the kind of human we want on the team. You didn't balk when you had to kill that kid or freak out when you stumbled into Wonderland. No, you stayed strong. You're one of us now, Cat McKenzie."

Although I was shaking my head, I was also secretly pleased that I was being accepted like this. All my life, I felt like I hadn't been, except by Mrs. Brown.

"All right, that's enough, Brax," Sawyer growled as he came into the room behind me. I turned around to face him. He studied me with cool disinterest, no doubt seeing the bruising on my neck, the cuts on my face and neck, and the dark crescents under my eyes.

I tried to piece together the image of the man who had taken care of me last night and the truth about what he was. I hadn't been lying when I'd said I didn't care what flavor of supe he was. I didn't. What I couldn't connect the dots on was the two sides of Sawyer.

Breaking into my thoughts, he said, "Let's go. There was a report of a vampire attack at a convenience store overnight."

I bobbed my head and followed him, hesitating a step when we got outside. My truck was gone, nothing but a crumpled ball of steel, which left us only one way to get around.

"You're insane if you think I'm getting on there." I pointed at his motorcycle.

He threw a spare helmet at me. "There's no other way to get there."

I cursed the department's lack of vehicles for PIG. "I'll take the bus."

He blew out an exasperated breath. "Just get on, pussy cat."

Resenting the name, and resenting that I liked it more when he said it, I slid the helmet onto my head and walked over to the bike. Sawyer sat astride, kicking the peg to get the engine started. I waited until his signal before sliding on behind him. I fixed my hands to his shoulders, but he repositioned them around his waist. I flexed my fingers, meeting the strong muscles of his stomach.

"Slide closer," he said, his voice coming directly through a speaker in the helmet. "Keep your good arm tight around my waist and hang on. I'll go as slow as I can."

"I hate you," I murmured, and his warm laughter filled the helmet a moment later.

"No, you're enjoying groping me right now."

I snorted but didn't deny it. He revved the engine, pushed the kickstand up, and we were off. He weaved through the streets of Buxton, flowing in between cars and trucks, making his movements seem like art rather than necessity. We didn't catch any traffic lights, and it was only fifteen minutes later that we drove into the parking lot of one of the ubiquitous twenty-four-hour mini marts that dotted the streets of Buxton.

"How was that?" Sawyer asked when he shut off the engine and put the bike back onto its stand.

"Horrifying."

"Horrifying because you liked it so much?"

"I miss my truck."

I began to fumble with the strap on the helmet, but he pushed my hands out of the way and undid it for me. Sliding the helmet off, he placed it onto the seat of the bike and looked at me. His fingers skimmed over the bruising on my neck where the bite was still fresh enough to sting. I winced.

"How are you feeling?"

I narrowed my eyes at him. "Why are you asking me now and being so sweet?"

He dropped his hands. "Sweet? What do you mean?"

"Oh, come on. You were playing it all cool in the office, and now that we're alone, you're fussing over me like a mother hen."

He quirked a brow at me. "Are you trying to tell me you don't like me fussing?"

Nope. It was quite the opposite. I was enjoying the hell out of it. But he was my partner, and there were boundaries we had to respect. I stepped away, putting some more space between us. "We should go in there and speak to the clerk."

Great deflection, Cat.

"Yeah, we should." His eyes drifted down to my waist. "Reaver not with you?"

"He was this morning." I shrugged my good shoulder. I had to figure out the pattern with him.

Reaching into his under-arm holster, he pulled out my side arm. "You might want this back then. Fully loaded, and I cleaned it for you too."

I placed it into the holster and clipped it in. "Thanks." He was being sweet, and it was shoving me off-balance. I had to get myself back on track. I jerked my chin at the E-Z-Mart. "Okay, so what happened here exactly?"

"Sanjeet Kapur reported a young boy wandering around his shop at two o'clock this morning. When Kapur approached the kid, he attacked, but Kapur fought him off."

"How? Those little bastards are strong."

"I don't know. That's why we're here to find out."

Following Sawyer inside, I tried to think of some good questions to ask Mr. Kapur. The main one I wanted to know was how in the hell did he fight off a baby vampire? I'd grappled with them and they are inhumanly strong, especially given their size.

The minimart was just as I imagined it would be. Row after row of snack foods guaranteed to give any pot smoker their munchie hit. Two out of the four walls were floor-to-ceiling fridges filled with everything from milk to soda to that manufactured blood source that had just been put on the market by a well-known drug company.

"Mr. Kapur?" Sawyer asked as he approached the raised front counter.

"Yes?"

Sanjeet Kapur was a Sikh. His ocean-blue E-Z-Mart polo shirt complimented his warm apricot colored dastar, the steel bracelets on his wrists jangling melodically as he moved. His long beard had flecks of gray in it, and I figured anyone who worked at a twenty-four-hour stop and rob like this would have more than their fair share of gray hair.

"I'm Detective Sawyer Taylor." Gesturing to me, he added, "And this is my partner, Officer Cat McKenzie. We're from PIG, and we're here to ask you some questions about what happened last night."

His dark brown eyes lit up. *Yes, the cavalry had arrived.* He walked around the counter and joined us on the main floor. Shaking our hands, he said, "What would you like to know?"

Pulling out his phone, Sawyer started the recording app and got down to business. "What time did your shift start yesterday?"

"I was here from five o'clock, like normal."

"How long are the shifts?" I asked.

"Twelve hours. My normal shift is five a.m. to five p.m., but my replacement didn't show up yesterday, so I stayed on."

"What does your boss have to say about those hours?" I asked.

He smiled, and I saw the younger man he used to be. "I am the boss, although my wife will be upset with me for working more than twelve hours. She worries."

"I don't suppose what happened last night filled her with comfort either." I glanced around the store, looking at the door and the corners of the ceilings as Sawyer continued his questions.

"What time did the young boy come in?"

"It was a little after two o'clock."

"Are you sure?"

He nodded. "Check the security footage. The controls are behind the counter. Just go around through the door there." He pointed to the end of the counter.

Sawyer nodded to me, and I did as he asked, finding myself on the raised platform. I looked out over the counter and saw that my view of things was actually amazing. From this height, whoever was working could see what people had in their hands, or whether they were carrying a weapon.

Ducking down, I found a computer monitor where I could see real-time black and white versions of Mr. Kapur and Sawyer. I glanced to my left to see the camera that was streaming, then watched the pattern.

Back left corner. Back right corner. Front right corner. Directly in front of the doors. The front left corner camera was just a dummy. I'd heard about it being done before. A lot of places only had one camera and placed dummy ones around the store in order to save money. Having all but one was strange though.

Using the keyboard, I scrolled the footage back to two o'clock that morning and hit play. A kid—or what looked like a kid—strolled casually inside. Dressed in jeans, a jacket and a sweet set of kicks he walked directly up to two-o'clock-Sanjeet and talked to him for a moment. Sanjeet, who had been stocking some shelves, stood up, towering above the child. The kid looked directly into the back, left corner camera, winked, then attacked without warning.

I would give Mr. Kapur credit—he was an absolute kick-ass fighter. I watched the pair of them grappling, the baby vampire wrapped around Sanjeet's upper body. It looked as if the vamp was trying to get them to the floor, where he could dominate. Whether Mr. Kapur knew that or not, he didn't let his attacker do that.

I pressed my face closer to the video when there was a faint glow coming from under Sanjeet's shirt. It got brighter and brighter, and the vampire was reacting. It tried to claw at his chest, but Sanjeet was raining down punches on him.

"Such a badass," I muttered under my breath.

Full respect to Sanjeet and his mad skills.

Eventually, the vamp just disappeared. One minute, he was there. The next, he was gone. I rewound that bit and played it back, frame by frame. That's when I realized he didn't just disappear, he moved so quickly it was just a blur. To the naked eye, it looked as if he'd poofed from existence.

When I stood up again, Sawyer and Mr. Kapur were still talking.

"What did you see?"

I gave him the run down, leaving out the part where the vampire actually winked at the camera before launching his attack.

"I must say, Mr. Kapur, I am *very* impressed with your fighting skills."

The older man blushed. "Thank you. It's been so long since I've had to use them."

"Right before the vampire fled, there was a glow from under your shirt. Do you know what happened?"

Reaching into the top of his shirt, Sanjeet pulled out a necklace with a gold Khanda pendant hanging from the bottom. It consisted of three swords, with a circle around the middle weapon.

"The circle or Chakra surrounding the Khanda is a metaphor

for the eternal God," he told me.

"It's a symbol of your faith." I glanced at Sawyer, and he nodded.

"Symbology carries a lot of power in the supernatural world. This Khanda would have the same effect as any Christian symbol, or any other religion for that matter."

"Where did you learn to fight, Mr. Kapur?" I asked, because I had to know.

He puffed out his chest a little, standing taller. "Twenty-fourth Battalion, Sikh Regiment. I retired in 2001."

I grinned at him. "You've still got it."

Bowing in thanks, he smiled back at me.

"All right, I think we have everything we need," Sawyer announced. "If we have any additional questions, I'll be sure to get in contact, Mr. Kapur."

"Thank you both for coming."

As we walked from the minimart, Sawyer murmured, "What did you find out from the surveillance tapes?"

"That Mr. Kapur is a *badass*."

"Anything else, other than hero worship?"

"Jealousy doesn't suit you, Sawyer," I said sweetly. "But yeah." I took the helmet he handed me and slid it over my head. As soon as Sawyer had his on too, I heard the coms crackle to life in my ear. "The fangy bastard winked at the camera before he attacked."

He swung his leg over the motorcycle and got into position. "Winked?"

I slid on behind him, wrapping my arm around his waist. "Winked. How many cameras do you think are in that store?"

"Maybe one functional one. The rest are probably dummies."

"Nope. He has five cameras. Only the front left is a dummy. The vampire looked directly at the camera that was on the cycle and winked right before he attacked."

He started the engine, and I scooted even closer. Easing out of the parking lot, he didn't talk again until we were on the road. "Okay, so it was premeditated."

"You're goddamn right it was. I don't know why Kapur was the victim, maybe it was just bad fucking luck, but he was. The E-Z-Mart, however, was not a coincidence."

"How do you figure?"

"It's just within our jurisdiction, right? One more block over, and it becomes Reynard PD's problem."

"Right." Sawyer's agreement of my assessment didn't fill me with confidence. "But why? Why attack anyone? Whoever is making these kids is creating them, then kicking them out of the nest right away. They have no idea of the rules."

"Or they're creating them to break the rules…"

"What do you mean?" Sawyer slowed the bike as he approached a red light. "What are you thinking?"

"I'm thinking what if these baby vamps are being made on purpose? Not a late nineties Britney, 'Oops I Did it Again' kind of thing, but an actual reason."

"And what would that reason be?"

I shook my head, feeling like the answer was just out of my

reach. "I don't know."

He touched my knee. "We'll figure it out, pussy cat."

My stomach lurched when he accelerated once more, blowing past the oncoming traffic almost recklessly. When we arrived back at the station, we walked back into the office.

"I've sent you the voice clip," Sawyer said, just before I heard the notification ping on my phone. "Would you mind taking notes while I go and follow up some other leads?"

If it meant I didn't have to get on the back of Sawyer's motorcycle again, I'd take his clear dismissal of me. Taking a seat at my desk, I plugged my AirPods into my ears and began typing.

WHEN I FINALLY FINISHED THE REPORT, ALONG WITH A DOZEN other things Sawyer kept passing off to me, it was just ticking over six p.m. I tilted my head from one side to the other to loosen the kink that had formed from hunching over my keyboard. Sawyer had been at his desk sporadically throughout the afternoon, but always disappeared before I could ask him what was happening next in our investigation.

He was finally back.

"Any developments I need to know about?"

"Yeah," he replied, tapping something out on his keyboard without looking at me. "Go home. Get changed. I'll be picking you up in an hour and a half."

"Why?"

He turned to me. "I got a call from Alistair. His mistress agreed to see us tonight."

I wanted to whine, *'More vampires?'* but held my tongue in check. See? I was learning. "Okay. What should I wear?"

"Something that covers the bite. If they see you've been taken from, they'll think you're easy pickings."

"Got it. Don't show the steak to the hungry dog."

"And wear your hair down."

"Why?"

"It'll help cover up your neck a little more."

Hey, if it saved me from becoming a vampire snack, I was all for it. "Got it. Anything else?"

"Yeah. Come with me."

I followed him into the weapons room, my fingers getting all twitchy when I thought about all the mischief I could get up to in here. Sawyer grabbed a leather holster then picked up four wooden stakes.

"Bring these with you."

I eyed them speculatively. "Won't they strip us of weapons?"

His mouth titled up in a grin. "Of that I have no doubt, but I'm hoping Reaver will be able to work his magic on them."

I returned his grin. "You wicked bastard."

He looked at the sling. "Think you could go without this tonight?"

Glancing down, I took stock of how my body felt. My shoulder was still sore, but the pain meds were good, making the pain a dull throb rather than an all-out bellow. "Why?"

"I don't want you to have weaknesses in front of them. Vampires are a dangerous enemy to have."

13

I pulled at the neck of the black turtleneck sweater and scratched at my chewed-on throat. It was beginning to itch, which meant it was beginning to heal. I had to take that as a win. With a sigh, I looked at my reflection and wondered if I'd done enough. Coupled with my sweater, I managed to pull on a pair of black skinny jeans and my motorcycle boots. The harness that would carry the stakes was crisscrossed over my chest, bisecting my breasts and making them look weird. I shrugged. Nobody would be staring at my breasts.

I was covered in black from head to toe, and even though I looked like an emo-goth circa 1990, my bright teal hair certainly pulled me out of any emotional tail-spin.

Right at seven-thirty, there was a knock on my door. Sawyer stood on my doorstep wearing an almost identical outfit—he'd just added a black leather riding jacket.

"Did you get your outfit from *Oh shit, we're meeting vampires tonight* too?" I asked.

He ran his eyes down my body, and I sucked in a breath. When he finally returned his eyes to my face, his gaze simmered with heat. "Are you ready?"

I managed to nod. "Almost. I just need to get these stakes strapped in."

"Let me give you a hand." Sawyer helped me position the smooth ash wood, his fingers brushing against mine every so often. I tried to ignore the way that made me feel. It helped to remember that he was an incubus and he could literally create those feelings of lust with no more than a well-timed smile.

I strapped Reaver to my back using another holster Sawyer had given me and touched the glyph of my freaking face to will it away.

Outside, it was a dark night. The new moon was doing sweet fuck all to illuminate anything, which wasn't a problem until we hit the city limits and were plunged into hick country.

"This is where the kiss lives?" I asked through the comms.

"This is where the mistress said we could meet with her. I doubt she'd allow cops into her actual place of residence."

I looked around the dark landscape, seeing nothing but murky, vague shapes of barns and trees. "Well, if she was going for creepy, hashtag Nailed-It."

"It'll be fine. Alistair will be there as our liaison."

"Not filling me with warm and fuzzies, Sawyer. In fact, I'm

getting filled with the opposite."

He patted my knee. "Trust me, pussy cat, I wouldn't let anything happen to you."

"You let me wander into Wonderland."

His abs flexed under my hands as he laughed. "I was in a shipping container nine feet in the air. I didn't even know what you were doing."

I sighed, hoping he heard how put out I was. "I'm like a child, Sawyer. If I'm not constrained in one of those weird tether things parents put on their kids, then I'm going to just wander off."

He laughed again, and I smiled. I liked it. I had a feeling he didn't laugh too much.

It only took another ten minutes before he slowed the bike and drove through a pair of stone plinths with carved gargoyles on the top. The avenue was tree lined and long, and when the house came into view, I thought we'd maybe traveled to Mississippi because it was Antebellum and plantation house all over. Sawyer parked his bike, and just as we lost the helmets, Alistair appeared at the top of the grand house's wraparound porch stairs.

"I see you didn't get lost."

I glanced around. "Is your mistress reliving the glory days of being a plantation owner?"

The vampire laughed. "No, she just has an appreciation for Neoclassical architecture."

"Top marks for her. Although, if she wanted to actually *blend* in around here, she'd have to seriously downgrade the house to a banged-up trailer."

"Humans can't see the property. Well, they can see the gates, but at the end of the driveway, there's nothing there but a field."

I wanted to scream *'How in the hell was that possible?!'* but then I remembered I was but a puny, weak-minded human and the supernatural community was more advanced than us and scary as fuck. "Noted."

"How is she?" Sawyer asked, coming to stand beside me. Showing a united front, good for him.

"Angry."

"About?"

"The attacks last night."

"Attacks?" I asked, stressing the plurality. I looked at Sawyer, who gave me an indecipherable look. To Alistair, I demanded, "How many were there?"

He shrugged his shoulders and smiled wickedly. "You really don't want to know."

I hated supes. No, correction—I hated vamps. They were so snooty and holier than thou. I got that they may have been on this earth for a lot longer than I had, but they were a bunch of douche bunnies who were too smug for my liking.

"Let's get on with it," Sawyer pressed. He walked up the stairs, and after a moment of hesitation, I followed. I didn't like the idea of being inside a house I had no idea how to get around in with a bunch of fangers who wanted nothing more than to strip me of my hemoglobin.

Call me paranoid, but there it was.

Alistair flowed into the house like he was made of water, waiting until both Sawyer and I were inside before slamming the door. Something heavy and metallic slid into place, and I jerked around to see a foot-thick steel crosspiece barring the only easy entry and exit point. I guessed defenestration it was.

"That's a bit much, isn't it?" I jerked my chin in the direction of the door. "It's not like this is a crime hotspot."

Alistair indulged me with an innocent-looking smile, flashing his fangs. "Speaking of crime, I have to ask you to take off your weapons before you see my mistress."

He snapped his fingers, and two more vampires appeared, startling me. My heart began to pound, fear kicking the bastard against my ribs in an effort to get them both the hell out of there. I tried to stay cool, to follow Sawyer's lead. He opened up his arms like he was being frisked by security at the airport, looking cool and nonplussed.

I felt exposed, like I was going to lose my arsenal of security blankets. Sawyer did say they would remove weapons from me. I'd just been languishing in misguided hope that it wouldn't happen.

"Spread your arms and legs."

Turning my head, I stared at the vampire who had spoken to me. He looked like he'd also stepped from the set of *Interview with the Vampire*, the look complete with a frilly cream shirt and sapphire blue cravat. His vest and jacket both had gold embroidered thread woven into the fabric, the shape of a serpent appearing in every single curve and whirl. He gave me a predatory smile as he ran his hands over my shoulders, patting me down.

"Get handsy and you lose your life," I said to him sweetly.

With a snarl, he continued working his way down my body. The first thing to go was my gun. I didn't care so much about that one. I heard guns weren't all that effective against vampires anyways. I sucked in a breath, though, when he got to the stakes on my chest. He eyed the holster.

"Forget to put something in this?" he asked, sliding a finger beneath the leather to indicate the empty holster.

I jolted in surprise but played it cool. "Oh, I did?" I feigned. "I guess that was stupid."

I caught Sawyer's smirk at my words.

"It might be the last mistake you make, *human*."

"Promises, promises," I replied.

I was left with all four stakes and Reaver. I would kiss that damn sword if we got out of this alive. The two lackeys finished frisking us, then dumped my sidearm as well as Sawyer's small arsenal of a gun, half a dozen knives, and a stake onto the table. The pair of vampires disappeared as quickly as they'd arrived, and I was left with a distinct case of vertigo.

Clearing my throat, I asked, "What's with the bar on the door?"

Alistair said, "The kiss sleeps here. Having someone come through that door during the day would be a disaster. This way."

I wanted to argue that it was evening and the vamps were awake right now, but I shut my mouth. The fact that the bar was on the door wasn't the point. The point was Roxanne Monroe was flexing her dominance and power, and I wasn't about to cry foul.

I half expected Alistair to take us into a parlor where sweet tea would be served. Alas, no such luck. Instead, the vampire led us down a long hallway before opening a door that revealed a void of darkness.

"I'll wait out here," I told Sawyer, eying the descending stairs that disappeared into nothingness. There was no way I was going to go down there when I had no idea what was waiting. It was like the start of every fucking slasher movie I'd ever seen.

"It's not safe to be left on your own," Alistair pointed out. "There are some vampires here that will claim they didn't hear the mistress's edict to do no harm to you and Sawyer. But if you come with me and stay by my side, on my honor, no harm shall come to you."

I hated this. I hated that I had to trust a vampire with my safety while we were in the belly of the beast, but what other choice did I have? Swallowing hard, I gestured Sawyer to go ahead of me while I took the rear position. I reached out for the handrail, the metal cold as ice against my palm. My necklace started to heat up a bit, just a little warning, and I clung to it. Lower and lower we went, the basement stairs defying logic and the laws of physics it seemed. Water dripped somewhere deeper into the darkness, but I focused on a flicker of what I thought could be torchlight up ahead.

"You know, electricity is a wonderful invention," I said offhandedly.

Alistair chuckled. "Vampires don't need light to see in the dark."

"Fantastic," I deadpanned. "I was thinking more about your visitors."

When we finally reached the bottom of the stairs, it felt as if we'd been walking for hours. More torches flickered in gothic wrought iron sconces on the walls, making the large cave we were standing in glow with warm yellow light. The walls flickered, the flames dancing on its smooth surface.

"I have a feeling we're not in Kansas anymore, Toto," I whispered to myself.

There was a circle of vampires waiting for a us, and I wondered briefly whether there was another collective noun for a group of vampires. A seduction? A flock? I giggled, then sobered almost immediately. But come on, a flock of vampires? I got an image of white feathered birds begging for scraps at the beach. Then I imagined them as a late seventies band with a penchant for Aqua Net. I could go on.

"Something funny?" Sawyer asked softly.

"Just amusing myself," I replied. "It stops me from having a full-blown panic attack."

"I suppose laughter is better than screaming."

"Is that what you say to all your dates?"

Sawyer blinked at me, then turned to face the bigger threat, because although I liked to *think* of myself as a threat, I was clearly not one. I was five foot four, so I could barely scare a kindergartener.

"Sawyer Phineas Taylor," someone purred in a throaty voice. I jerked my head up to see a blonde woman stepping away from the circle of vampires, approaching us. She was wearing a dress that matched the era of the house, all frills, corsets, and petticoats. Did she not realize it was the twenty-first century yet?

"Roxanne Monroe, how nice to finally meet you."

She held out her hand to him, and he kissed it, keeping his eyes on her face. "I've heard so many things about you."

"All good, I hope." With a wicked smile that matched the wicked gleam in her blue-lilac eyes, she turned her attention to me. My necklace grew a little hotter, and I sensed it was glowing. Thank God I had a thick sweater on to hide that fact.

I shifted uneasily on my feet as Roxanne sniffed me like I was a fine dinner… or a bag of blood. I guessed I was a glorified bag of blood. "And who is this delectable treat you've bought?"

"Officer Cat McKenzie," I told her. "Sawyer's partner."

Roxanne turned her attention back to Sawyer. "Well, isn't she delightful?" she drawled.

"See?" I asked him.

"It was a rhetorical question," Sawyer shot back, never taking his eyes off the mistress of the kiss. "I assume Alistair has enlightened you on our current situation?"

She waved her long elegant hand through the air, then spun around, her skirts and petticoats kicking out around her ankles. "Yes, yes. Baby vampires running amok in Buxton."

She glided to a chaise lounge I hadn't seen pressed against one of the cave walls. Was this place where they hung out when they were entertaining, or was this their full-time living quarters?

"Correct. I was just wondering whether you could share some

more information with us."

She laughed throatily. Damn, talk about a phone sex voice. "Why would I help PIG, or *humans* for that matter?"

I bristled at the tone of disgust she used when she said 'humans.' I understood we were no longer the apex predator, but we didn't need it rubbed in our faces all the time.

"They're your food source," Sawyer countered. "Why wouldn't you want to protect them from a foreign vampire?"

"*Foreign?*" she asked, testing the word. "Is that what Ali told you?" She fixed the other vampire with a deadly stare.

Beside me, Alistair shifted from foot to foot. Really, it was quite unbecoming for a vampire his age to fidget. "I told them he was an acquaintance of yours from Italy, Mistress."

"True enough," Roxanne replied in a menacing tone. "But not quite the truth." She looked around the cave, her gaze settling on every single one of her vampires before finally landing on me. I forced myself to stand still. She continued, "I knew him in Italy, but he was more my enemy than a friend."

"Why did you let him come into your territory then?"

Roxanne narrowed her eyes at Sawyer, the temperature in the cave plummeting. "Leave us."

I jumped at the command, but it wasn't aimed at me or Sawyer. As the rest of the vampires moved away, I realized she was giving us privacy…or she was trying to hide something from her minions.

"You too, Alistair," Roxanne added when he remained at my side. I glanced over my shoulder at him, startled to see his green eyes glowing faintly. There was a heartbeat of time where they simply stared at one another, both his and Roxanne's expressions shifting ever so slightly as if they were having a mind-to-mind conversation. "Go," she finally commanded.

Ali bent at the waist, bowing to his mistress. "As you wish." The words were benign, but the anger in his clipped tone gave away his feelings about being dismissed.

Once Ali was gone, Roxanne said, "Can I get you something to eat or drink?"

Sawyer said, "We're fine."

She sighed, but the action looked forced, like she hadn't done it in a long time. "Draco Vasilli is his name, and I don't know why he's here."

"Yet you allow him to stay," he said. "Why?"

The glare she gave him made me flinch, but Sawyer absorbed the blow effortlessly. "I don't *allow him* anything," she snipped. "He is more powerful and *older* than me. Therefore, I cannot stop him from doing as he wants in my territory."

"You have a kiss at your disposal though. Why not use your force?"

"Because Draco's particular skills lie in manipulations of the mind. He can force anyone to bend to his will or make them believe any number of illusions he's spun up to benefit himself."

"Anyone?" I asked.

She turned her Elizabeth Taylor eyes on me, lilac flames bursting life. "Anyone. Draco is a plague among our species. He comes into a place, takes what he wants, then leaves it ravaged and barren."

"It sounds like Draco has been a bad vampire," I muttered.

"He has," she replied in a smooth purr, effortlessly standing up from the chaise. She prowled toward me, coming to an abrupt stop less than a foot away from me. "And if it's in your power to remove him from this earth, I believe I would find myself in your debt."

"And how are we supposed to do that?"

Her gaze drifted down to my décolletage. "I know of a witch who can help."

"Great, there are witches too?" I asked, getting blank looks from both Sawyer and Roxanne. I shrugged, unrepentant. "This has been an enlightening few days."

Roxanne smiled like a viper. "Oh, you have no idea what else is out there."

I held up my hand to stop here. "All I cared about was unicorns, and apparently, they're not real."

"They were in the Dark Ages," the vampire replied, licking her fingers. "Absolutely delicious to eat."

I blanched. That was like watching *Bambi* and then saying, 'Let's have venison for dinner!' Argh, I felt sick.

"Alistair will have the witch's details for you. If you rid this earth of Draco Vasilli, Cat McKenzie, I will be at your disposal whenever you need me."

I didn't know what to say. It was like having a tame tiger on standby. Thankfully, Sawyer saved me from awkwardness.

Bowing ever so slightly to Roxanne, he said, "Come on, Cat."

I followed behind him, cursing when more sconces came to life on the walls with a burst of flame. They illuminated the way up the stairs, revealing well-worn stone with dips in the center where centuries of foot traffic had worn them away. When we got back to the top, I screamed when Alistair appeared out of thin air.

I clutched at my chest. "Jesus *Christ*! Can you make a sound when you move? Please?"

The vampire gave me an amused look before saying to my partner, "The mistress said you needed this." He handed him a piece of thick, folded paper.

Sawyer tucked the information into the inside pocket of his jacket. "Thanks."

With a nod, Ali added, "Your weapons are where you left them on the front table."

We re-armed ourselves, then left the house. I practically crawled onto the back of Sawyer's bike in an effort to get us out of there even sooner. I wasn't ashamed that I clung to him as he drove back down the driveway and out onto the main road, the headlights on his bike the only thing chasing the shadows away.

"When do we have to go and see the witch?" I asked.

Please say never. Please say never.

"I'll call them tonight, but I don't think it'll be until tomorrow if I'm being honest."

"I like honesty."

He chuckled.

14

"We're not done yet. We're going out."

I glanced up at Sawyer. "Now?" He opened his mouth, and I cut him off. "I know, crime doesn't sleep." Heaving a sigh, I stood up. We'd literally only come back to the office for a minute to divest ourselves of the stakes. I'd been slumped down in my chair for precisely thirty-five of those glorious sixty seconds. The office was empty, but not the building itself. There were still about two dozen cops working in other departments, all *not* getting involved in supernatural work.

"Where are we going?"

"The witch's place. She returned my call and said she could meet us now."

I stared forlornly at the clock on the wall. "It's almost nine."

"Oh, I'm sorry, did you have somewhere else to be? Got a hot date?"

I went to cross my arms, but stopped when my shoulder screamed at me. Settling my hands into my lap, I said, "And what if I did? I certainly wouldn't be telling you."

He leaned closer to me, making my heart rate lurch. I did my best to ignore his dark chocolate and smoky whisky scent. His sinful mouth curled up in the corner. "You don't have a date. Come on. The sooner we get this done, the sooner we can all go home."

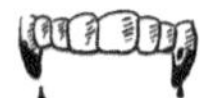

THE WITCH, AS IT TURNED OUT, LIVED IN MY BUILDING. I WAS definitely going to have to look for somewhere else to live. On the plus side, I only had to climb one flight of stairs to get home. Hello, silver lining.

Sawyer knocked on the door with all the authority of a cop on a mission. It opened up a moment later, and the woman on the other side looked like she hadn't bathed in a month. She kind of smelled like that too. Her dirty gray hair was loose around her face, but there were clumps of it that stuck up at odd angles. She couldn't have been any older than fifty, but the way her shoulders rolled forward made it seem as if she'd seen a few more years on this earth than that. She would've been beautiful thirty years ago, but that beauty had long withered away.

"Ms. Flynn? Sharyn Flynn?" Sawyer asked.

She bobbed her head, her greasy hair sliding into her eyes. She shoved it out of the way with an impatient noise and narrowed her cool blue eyes at us.

"Who are you?"

"Alistair sent us," he replied. "I'm Detective Taylor and this is my partner, Officer McKenzie. We were hoping you could help us."

"Cops?"

"PIG," Sawyer replied, reaching inside his jacket and pulling out a thick envelope, no doubt stuffed with cash. Had PIG foot the bill for the informant, or was this money from Sawyer's own pocket? "For your trouble."

She reached out with greedy fingers and stepped away from the door. I looked longingly in the direction of the elevators, wondering if I could simply go home and get the report later. Judging by the glare Sawyer gave me, that would be a hard *no*.

It was a struggle not to throw my arm over my nose when I stepped into the apartment. It smelled of blue cheese that had been left on a radiator for a week. I knew the smell because I'd 'accidently' done that to an ex-boyfriend in college. What? The bastard had cheated on me. That stunt was performed by restrained, past Cat.

I wasn't nearly as forgiving now.

Layered with that blue cheese funk, there was smell of unwashed bodies and putrefaction. I wondered if the super knew what she was and what she was doing, but I'd bet my favorite unicorn statue that she was killing puppies and kittens in here too.

The layout was identical to mine—kitchen on the left, living room in front of me. To the right was a short hallway to the bathroom, bedroom, and a small storage closet. Unlike my apartment, the walls were painted a dark gray, almost black, and everything was coated in some kind of oily film.

"What do you need? Alistair was spare with the details," the witch said impatiently, gesturing to the couch. Both Sawyer and I shook our heads. It looked like one of those sofas that was deep enough to hold you in place if you needed to get up unhindered. In other words, they were a fucking death trap.

"There's a vampire turning kids. We need to find him before any more children are killed or turned needlessly."

She clacked her yellow-stained teeth and cocked her head to the side. "I've heard stirrings of vampires."

"Can you help?"

"Yes, but I need something either the vampire, or one of the vampire's progenies has touched in the last twenty-four to forty-eight hours." She stared directly at my throat, which was still covered by the neck of my sweater.

"Why do you need that?" I asked, resisting the urge to touch the spot her eyes lingered on.

"I can create a tracking spell, but I need to have something organic from the person you're trying to track. If he's creating vampires, any saliva or blood from one of them will do what I need it to do."

From the corner of my eye, I saw Sawyer look at me pointedly. The bastard. He probably knew this, yet he couldn't have given me a fucking warning?

I shrugged awkwardly out of my jacket and, despite feeling vulnerable, peeled the turtleneck sweater off too. "Fine. Yes, one of his vampires bit me. How is this supposed to work?"

The witch's eyes lit up when she saw my opal necklace against my chest on the outside of my black tank top. A small hiss escaped her throat, and I drew the opal back under the fabric. She was going all *my precious* on it and freaking me out even more than I already was.

As soon as the stone wasn't visible, she gave herself an avian shake and said, "I need something personal of yours. The necklace perhaps?"

"How about fucking no?" I replied defensively, folding my arms over my chest.

The woman shrugged like it was no big deal, but I saw the desperation in her eyes. "Blood will suffice." Her words were cool and clipped.

"Ooo, another hard limit of mine. Sorry."

"Cat," Sawyer said softly. I glared at him. "This is our only chance."

"I highly doubt that," I shot back. I didn't enjoy being backed into corners. I tended to get bitchy.

"Maybe you're right, but how many more baby vampire attacks do we need to go and investigate? If we have a chance to catch this guy, shouldn't we?"

I digested his words. I didn't like it. I didn't like that I seemed to be the one sacrificing everything here. My truck. My promise not to murder children. My staunch belief that all supernatural beings were evil monsters. Now, I was being asked to give up my blood. All so that Sawyer could catch a vampire.

"You will pay for this, Sawyer Taylor. I swear it."

"Noted," he replied. "Thank you."

"Don't thank me yet. You have no idea what kind of revenge I have in mind. I can be very creative." Turning to the witch, I asked, "You can take one drop of blood."

She shook her head. "Not enough. Too weak. Not enough," she repeated. "A deep cut. Deep blood."

"Wow, I didn't think you could get any creepier," I muttered. "Okay, but you don't make the cut. I do."

Her greedy eyes gleamed. "Fine." Looking down, she searched the coffee table in front of her. Shoving an old newspaper out of the way, she held up a dagger that was crusted with dried… something. I stared at it. Hard. What the actual fuck was that?

"Use this," Sawyer said helpfully, handing me one of his daggers.

I began shaking my head. "I've seen what they do. I'm not using that on my arm."

"Trust me?" he pressed, his eyes darting to the witch then back to me. "Take it."

Trust was a concept I struggled with, but I needed to trust my partner now. Nodding, I took the knife. The witch let out a soft little chuckle that had me looking frantically at Sawyer.

"There's no other way?" I desperately needed another way. Admittedly, I was as ignorant as ignorant got about the supernatural world, but I knew deep down that sharing blood was bad.

"Blood is power. Blood will create a strong spell. Powerful." The witch's muttering was doing absolutely nothing to make me feel better. Her ramblings just got creepier and creepier.

Forcing out a sigh, I placed the tip of the knife against my arm and shut my eyes, sending the message to my brain that I needed to apply pressure. But after a minute, I was still in the same place… only my breathing was labored as fuck. Sawyer wrapped one of his warm hands around mine.

"Let me do it?" I cracked one eye open. He leaned in a little closer, keeping his words to me private. "I can take the pain away for you, if you'd let me?"

I nodded, because that sounded like the best fucking idea I'd ever heard. I gave the knife to him and dropped my free arm to my side.

He wrapped his warm, strong fingers around my other arm, holding me gently but firmly. With his thumb, he stroked the pulse point on my wrist for a minute. I relaxed into the sweeping sensation, trying to let my thoughts drift away from what was happening right now. I had to stay sharp, alert.

"Deep breath," he murmured. "Keep your eyes shut. Don't move."

Sucking in a lungful of oxygen, I braced for the pain…

That never came. A small gasp escaped me as heat flooded my body. It wasn't heat from a fire. Rather, it was the heat that came from a lover's caress. I warmed all over, all thoughts of a witch taking my blood and vampires leaving my mind. All I could focus on was this warmth. I let out a groan when Sawyer skimmed my thigh with his fingertips. Granted, this was not how partners touched, but I found I didn't actually care right now.

He feathered his hand farther up the inside of my thigh, rubbing the seam of my jeans, sending sparks through me. I widened my stance, giving him the access he needed. God, I hoped he needed it because I wasn't ready for him to stop touching me like this. He applied more erotic pressure, playing, teasing, making me drip with desire. I had never felt this alive, this electrified, with barely a hint of foreplay before. I guessed bedding an incubus did have its perks.

I ground my pussy against the heel of his palm, begging for more—more friction, more touching, rougher touching. I wanted it all.

He laid his mouth against my arm, licking from my wrist to the crook of my elbow. If it were any other fool licking me, I would've told them to fuck off by now, but with Sawyer, I wanted to hold his head there forever. I decided then that he could do whatever the fuck he wanted to do with me and I would go along with it.

Willingly.

Sacrifice me on the altar of Sawyer's dick and sexual prowess, and I'd become his priestess.

"It's done," he whispered, and I opened my eyes. Blinked. Stared at the cut on my arm. It hadn't been his tongue on my skin, but the blade. Blood oozed out in thick wave, and the witch was there with a red Solo cup, scooping up what she could. I jerked back when she dipped her head and ran her tongue over the wound.

"Enough," Sawyer growled. "You have your payment. Do what we asked."

The witch smiled at me with blood-stained teeth and shuffled into the kitchen. I turned back to Sawyer, still too stunned to move.

He pulled a handkerchief out of his pocket and wrapped it around my arm. "This will have to do for now. I assume you have a first-aid kit in your apartment?"

Blink. That's all I could do. My brain felt fuzzy and thick, my thoughts coalescing slowly and without much sense. What had just happened to me?

Blink.

Blink.

I squeezed my legs together as an echo of an erotic throb pounded through my pussy. Sawyer's eyes had grown darker. He had a hand wrapped around my uninjured arm, holding me like he was worried I would bolt.

"We'll talk later," he said softly, brushing his fingers along my cheek.

I blinked again. Fuck, I had to get some other innate function going. Breathing! Oh, wait, I was already doing that. Crying? Nah, not in front of a witch I'd just met… and was potentially going to be running into in the building in the future. Because hooray for me.

The witch returned with a shard of mirror about an inch wide and three inches long, one end tapering off to a sharp point.

Sawyer demanded, "What's that?"

"A conduit."

"And what does it do?"

"I've bespelled the mirror so you can see what the vampire is seeing."

I cleared my throat, finally finding my voice. "Wow, that's just needle-in-the-haystack fantastic."

Sawyer coughed pointedly and held out his hand. "I'll take it."

The woman shook her head. "Her blood. Only she can see." She thrust the piece of mirror at me, and I reluctantly took it. As soon as my fingers touched the smooth surface, my skin seemed to sizzle. I pocketed the thing and hoped it didn't stab me in the ass.

The witch tittered to herself. "Powerful. Powerful. Watch them burn."

"Can we leave now?" I asked Sawyer, not even trying to hide my desperation to leave.

"Yes."

Without another word, we left the apartment while the witch got lost in her own head, muttering those same words over and over again.

"Never take me on a date like that again," I said to Sawyer as I rode the elevator up to my apartment.

He quirked an eyebrow at me. "That's what you call a date?"

I shrugged. "I haven't been out much. Plus…" I drifted off, letting my thoughts die. My partner didn't need to know about my sexual habits, although considering he nearly just got me off in front of a witch, maybe he already knew.

"Plus?"

"Oh, look, my apartment!" I exclaimed with way too much enthusiasm and volume. I opened up the door and walked in, not caring if Sawyer followed me in or not. After tonight, I think I wanted to be alone anyway.

"Where's the first aid kit?" he asked, shutting the door and bolting it.

"Bathroom." I placed the mirror shard on the table and plonked down onto the couch, staring at the blood-soaked handkerchief until he returned with the medical supplies.

"How does it feel?"

I jerked my head up and stared at him. How did *what* feel? If he was talking about the cut, I barely felt it. If he was talking about the echo of his touch? I was all up for exploring that further.

I erred on the side of caution. "Dull."

Lowering himself onto his knees, I watched him through half lidded eyes as he removed the handkerchief and cleaned the wound. It was a neat cut, one that would hopefully not scar. He didn't say anything for a long time, and neither did I, since I was still processing every fucked-up thing that had happened.

"I'm sorry."

"Not as sorry as you're going to be," I replied in a half-hearted sing-song voice.

"Not for the blood. I'm not sorry if that's how we can find this vampire. I'm sorry for the other thing."

I forced my eyes to widen, deciding to play dumb. "Other thing?"

"The distraction I provided?"

"You mean touching me?"

Sawyer shook his head, his gray eyes clear and unbeguiling. "Other than your arm, I didn't touch you," he replied.

What the hell was he talking about? As if my body wanted to scream at him that *it* remembered being touched, a bolt of lust shot through me. I shifted in my seat, the reality of his words sinking home. "You manipulated my mind into thinking…" Jesus, I couldn't even bring myself to say the words.

He nodded, never taking his eyes off his work. "I could see that you were terrified, and I needed to relax you. Believe me, I would never intentionally use my powers to influence you unless it was absolutely necessary." Dumping the bloody gauze onto the table, he opened up a bandage and some more non-stick pads. "I think you should know what species I am."

"You're an incubus," I told him. I shouldn't have enjoyed how much I'd clearly taken him by surprise, but I did. I felt like I was lost in this supernatural world, always the one with the wool pulled over her eyes, so it was nice to be on the other end, even if it was for something as small as this.

"How did you…? *Faline*," he growled.

"Yes, Faline, but don't be pissed off with her. Why didn't you tell me sooner?"

"Hold this." I pressed the non-stick pad in place as he unwound a little of the bandage. "I didn't tell you because I didn't want you to throw me under the fucking bus if we got into trouble."

"Buses aren't my style. I prefer taxis. Those drivers are savage." He stared at me, and I shrugged. "I know what you mean. I was a loose cannon. I'd watched my partner get murdered and didn't do a damn thing to stop it. Or help."

He nodded, still working the bandage around my forearm. "If you could do that to a human partner, I didn't want to think about what you would do to a supernatural one."

"I would never…" Pausing, I thought about the words I was about to say, about what I'd told Faline. "We're partners, Sawyer. You being an incubus doesn't change that."

"And you being human doesn't change that for me either," he replied softly, amusement glittering in his gray eyes.

"Are we bonding, Sawyer?"

His mouth flexed into a small smile, the one I knew showed his genuine amusement. "In our own strange way."

I sighed through my nose and said, "Okay, you're an incubus. So did you use your pussy-soaking whammy on me?"

I got a loud laugh that time. "Pussy-soaking whammy?" he asked.

"Yeah, you know, that thing you do to make women pant all over you. I saw the way that woman in the coffee shop reacted. She looked like she wanted to claw my eyes out for standing close to you." Eh, it was a stretch of the truth.

Sawyer looked confused, then when it finally dawned on him, he said, "That was you? The woman in front of me?"

I huffed. *Don't let it sting.* "Yeah. Am I so unforgettable?"

He had the good grace to look chagrined. "I don't know what to say. I went in there to get coffee. I was in a bad mood because I was getting a new partner and I'd lost the bet."

"Bet?"

"Yeah. We had a pool going about who they would send and who they would be assigned to. I got shafted twice."

I tried not to laugh. Really, I did. "All right, so bad mood Sawyer," I pressed, hurrying him on because thinking about him hating me made my chest hurt.

"Bad mood Sawyer equals slightly misdirected energy. I needed to feed before I met you, so I took a hit at the coffee shop. I didn't even notice who was there. All I knew was there were three women in there, and I needed something. That woman in line behind us and the barista were soaked for me. I could smell it. You, on the other hand…"

"Me?"

He stood up, collecting the gauze and packaging as he did, then disappeared into my kitchen. "You," he said as he returned, shivering. "You are something else."

"I have a feeling I'm not going to like what you're going to say next."

He sat down beside me on the couch, and I shifted my body around, facing him. My arm throbbed dully, and I held it on top of my leg carefully. I studied his face. He looked so torn, so I decided to save him from saying anything more.

"So with the witch, that was all in my head?"

He nodded. "I'm sorry if I overstepped."

I didn't care that he'd tapped my mind like an overripe watermelon. I hadn't been able to make the cut, so he did. If we caught the vampire now, it was because he was there to help me.

"I'll call it even if you tell me why you don't have fangs like Faline."

"Only female sex demons have fangs."

"Sex demons? Woah, I thought you said you were an incubus."

"I am. We're a species of sex demon—well, what humans call demons. For us, it's just a different race. You have black, Caucasian, Asian, and so on. We have our own classification system."

"All right, so females get fangs. What do male sex demons get? A twelve-inch dick? Orgasm-inducing cum? Your finger turns into a vibrator?"

He laughed, throwing his head back as he did. One point to me. I needed to lighten the mood. Seriously though, I knew he had the twelve-inch dick package when he'd gotten into the shower with me after the accident, but was there anything else?

"So, are we good? You know…" He gestured to my bandaged arm.

"Yeah, we're good. Although, now I kind of wished I'd used my necklace instead." I glared at the shard of mirror on the table.

"Oh?"

"Yeah. Less stabby," I replied absently.

He conceded my statement with a nod. "That is true. Although, I'm not sure your necklace would've worked."

"Why not?"

"I've noticed it glows sometimes."

I wrapped my hand around it protectively. I'd been told by my father never to take it off, that it would protect me as long as I was wearing it. "What's the theory?"

"I think it's been bespelled already." I digested his words, nodding to indicate he should go on. "Every time there's a supernatural around using their gifts, it glows. I noticed it when you were in Wonderland fighting Baba Yaga. Did it also happen in the coffee shop?"

I tried to piece it all together in my head, getting the timeline straight. "That was the first time it flared to life. Before that, I guess I never came into contact with anything supernatural…" I clutched at the stone a little more tightly, choosing to omit all the truth about all the other times it had glowed in warning after that. Had it really been bespelled? There was only one person I could think to ask, and that was Mrs. Brown. The only problem was, I had no idea where to find her. I frowned. I also couldn't remember what she looked like.

Sawyer stood up and stretched, the bottom of his sweater riding up with the movement. Unashamedly, I stared at the strip of skin he flashed. When he caught me staring, he gave me a lazy grin, then kissed me on the top of my head. "I'll see you tomorrow, pussy cat. Get some rest."

15

The next day was uneventful. All I did was go through voice clips and write reports. I had a sneaking suspicion Sawyer was taking it easy on me. I was good with that. My arm still throbbed from where the witch had taken her blood, and I wasn't sure my nerves could handle being on the back of Sawyer's bike again so soon.

I'd planned on getting a new truck over the weekend.

If the damn thing ever got here.

"Does time move differently in this department?" I asked Sawyer as he busied himself with something I couldn't see.

"What do you mean?"

"I mean, how is it only Thursday? I feel like I've been working here a year already."

Across the room, Faline laughed. She'd returned to her desk

after being out in the field for most of the day. "You think we have our own measurement of time? Our own supernatural Gregorian calendar?" It wasn't my most outlandish idea. She got up from her chair and sauntered over to me, her hips moving with serpentine grace.

"What are you doing tonight?"

I glanced over at Sawyer, who kept his eyes on his work, but tilted his head a little to the side to show he was listening. "Why?"

I had planned on seeing my therapist. After Sawyer had left last night, I'd kind of reached my breaking point. There was only so much supernatural horseshit I could shovel at a time, and my cart was full.

"It's my birthday. We're," she gestured to the whole room, "going out tonight to celebrate. I would like to you come."

I narrowed my eyes, asking, "Why?" again.

Faline perched on the edge of my desk and stared at me. "Because I like you, and I *think* we're friends?"

"What constitutes being a friend with a succubus?"

Pressing her abnormally long tongue between her teeth, she tapped her chin with a long-fingered nail in thought. "Being cool with me feeding off sexual energy while in my presence. Being okay with the fangs." She pointed at the dental hardware. "Being okay with what I am, and what my nature is."

I opened my mouth to protest, but then shut it. She was right. I was okay with all those things. When had that happened? I looked back over at Sawyer to find him actively listening now.

"Are you going?"

He shrugged, which could've meant yes or no.

"Sawyer can even pick you up if you want," Faline kindly offered, blowing my partner a kiss.

He growled but didn't deny it.

"Where are you going?"

"Slayke. Have you heard of it?"

"The supe club?"

"It's actually a supernatural sex club," Brax added helpfully from behind his desk.

I turned in his direction. "Are you going?"

He shook his head. "Nah. My mate would kill me if I left her alone all night with four kids and a newborn."

"You have kids?"

His responding grin practically lit up the room. "I do. Drae and I had another baby girl just over a month ago. We named her Willow."

Okay, so my heart went a little mushy with that declaration. I turned back to Faline. "Okay. What should I wear?"

"Something that'll bring all the boys to the yard," she purred. "Maybe you should come and get ready at my place."

"Gah. No. I am perfectly capable of choosing my own clothes."

The succubus pouted. "But it's my birthday, and you haven't gotten me anything."

"I've just given you airtime," I shot back, then sighed. "Fine. But this is it. No more freebies from Cat. Oh! And no leather, whips, chains, gimp masks, ball gags, or pink."

She threw her hands up into the air. "Well there goes my idea to put you in a cute pink pant suit ala *Legally Blonde.*"

"That's not funny." Beside me, Sawyer chuckled. "Traitor," I muttered.

Faline patted the top of my head before she walked away. "You can come home with me."

"I'm already shaking in my boots," I said to myself as I got back to work.

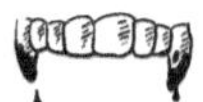

FALINE'S APARTMENT WAS NOT WHAT I WAS EXPECTING. IN FACT, I didn't know what I was expecting, but an open-planned, light-filled, and Hampton's style decor was not it.

"Don't you have any demon-y things?" I walked around the room, touching the shells and vintage nautical paraphernalia dotted around the walls. The rug beneath my bare feet felt expensive…and freaking amazing.

"Define demon-y things." Faline was in the galley kitchen, pulling some wine from the fridge. "Like torture devices?"

"Maybe." I spun to face her. "Or, I don't know… brimstone?"

She scrunched up her delicate nose. "Brimstone is disgusting. It stains the rugs, and that smell? Can't get it out at all."

"You sound like you've had first-hand experience."

She shrugged, brandishing a bottle at me. "Wine or something stronger?"

I walked toward the kitchen counter and perched on a bleached wood stool. "If I'm going to be playing dress-up Barbie, I'll need something a little stronger."

Her mouth flexed into a wicked smile. The bitch was going to enjoy this. She turned around and opened up a cupboard above the fridge. Without having to get a step. I hated her a little more. "I've got Goose, Jack, or Lag."

"Ooo, all my favorites. Lay some Jack on me."

She handed me a squat glass with ice and the bottle of Jack. "I have a feeling you'd like more than one drink."

I started pouring. "You got that right." I threw back the first mouthful, then poured another. "All right, I'm ready."

"For a firing line? Going to war?"

"Believe me, it kind of feels that way. No, I'm ready for you to recreate me." I scratched absently under the strap of my shoulder brace.

"Oh, honey, you say the sweetest things." Taking my free hand, she dragged me into her bedroom, which was just as light and airy as the rest of her apartment. She had an old fishing net on the wall, along with more nautical knick-knacks and enough throw pillows to bury a man.

She positioned me in front of a vanity mirror then pressed on my shoulders to make me sit. She began fussing with makeup trays and pots of things I couldn't even begin to identify.

"I'm going to make you look good enough to eat," she announced.

"Is that desirable when going to a sex club? There are things there that would actually eat me."

She gave me a wicked grin. "Only if you asked nicely."

Taking a deep breath, I waved my hand in front of me. "Carry on. I'll be here self-medicating."

With a throaty chuckle, she got to work.

An hour later, I barely recognized the face staring back at me. I hardly wore makeup. I didn't think it suited me, but it looked as if I was wrong, wrong, wrong about that. I was fucking hot. She'd left my hair loose in long teal waves that softened the harder edges of my face.

"I'd bang you," Faline announced with a grin. "You are so getting some action tonight."

"Action? I don't need any action."

"Why? Got a boyfriend stashed somewhere we don't know about?"

"No."

"Then you can enjoy yourself, and if someone offers you orgasms, you'll take them."

I turned back to stare at my reflection, my eyes running over the smoky makeup, the cat-eye liner, and the false lashes that I had to admit made me look fuckable now. "I'm not sure I can do it."

"Casual sex?"

I snorted. "Casual sex is fine."

"What is it then? Ah, the supernatural thing."

"It's not what you think," I blurted, swiveling around on the stool. "I don't think I'm as terrified of you guys any more, but others? I don't know. What if there are extra... appendages?"

She made of show of twisting her tongue around in a swirling motion. "Extra appendages are fun. Plus, if you don't want anyone to approach you, stick with me or Sawyer. We'll keep you safe." She waited until I nodded before saying, "Okay, time to get dressed."

"This is the part I'm scared about," I told her, following her into her *huge* walk-in closet. "This apartment is like a Tardis."

"Ah, a fellow Whovian." She began pulling dresses off the racks like this was a Nieman Marcus rather than her own personal wardrobe. I watched her with increasing trepidation. Eventually, she turned around and said, "Strip."

"Aren't you going to buy me dinner first?" I shot back with a grin, stripping out of my jeans and blouse.

"Cute panties," she commented, and I looked down at my unicorn print Victoria's Secret underwear.

"Thanks. I bought a life-time supply when they released this design."

"Badass. Unicorns are wicked. Step." She positioned the dress at my feet, and I stepped into the shimmering red fabric. It skimmed over my thighs and hips, finally coming to rest at my bust.

"Lose the bra and the shoulder brace if you can," Faline said absently as she walked around the back of me to zip up the dress. When it was done up, she stepped away, studying me.

"I like the color, but it's clashing with your hair," she said. "Next dress."

She got me into another three dresses before finally settling on a pair of leather pants that felt amazing against my skin and a black tank top that hit me just above my navel. Around my waist, she settled three leather bands that were nothing more than decorative. Finally, she slid me into a red leather jacket that finished at the waist and showed off my bare midriff.

"How does the shoulder feel?"

I shrugged. Honestly, I'd expected a lot more pain.

"Okay. What shoes do you want to wear?"

"My motorcycle boots?" I asked hopefully.

"Pfft, no. You're wearing fuck-me heels. It'll take the outfit to the next level."

As she searched for a pair of her heels for me to wear, and I secretly wondered how we both shared the same miniature shoe size, I asked, "Why did you decide against the dress? Not that I'm complaining, but I thought you were going to feminize me."

"I was, but I want you to be comfortable too. We're going to a place you've never been before, and I didn't want you hindered by fabric if something went wrong."

"Thanks for the foreshadowing," I joked. "But seriously, I really appreciate you considering my feelings."

"What are friends for?" she replied, stripping out of her work clothes. I leaned against the doorjamb, looking at the racks and racks of clothes she had. Some of them looked vintage, but then I remembered Faline was old and some of these outfits were probably originals.

"Holy shit, your back!" I hadn't meant to yell, but the words kind of popped out and were amplified. By a lot.

The succubus peered at me over her shoulder, the same shoulder that was covered in scars.

"You don't have a filter, do you?"

I waved away her comment. "Already established. They look like whipping scars?" She gave me a blank stare, and I asked, "What the hell happened to you?"

She shrugged and slid a black sheath dress over her head, the silky fabric covering her back and hiding it from view. The dress was full-length, but light enough that she could move easily. She slid on a pair of black stilettos—the bottoms painted a vibrant red that looked like blood.

Taking the cue that she didn't want to talk about it, I cleared my throat and asked, "So will you feed tonight?"

She smiled devilishly. "Oh yeah. Tonight, it's going to be like an all-you-can-eat buffet, and I'm going to *gorge* myself."

"Will you take someone home?"

"Only if someone takes my fancy. I've really been into fallen angels lately." She shivered. "Those fellas know how to spank a female."

"I can't unhear that," I drawled. "Thank you. Also, fallen angels are real?"

"Oh, sweet, sweet Cat. I forget that you're so ignorant sometimes. Fallen angels are a dichotomy of good and evil. Mostly evil, but they know how to make a female feel good."

"Remind me never to fuck a fallen angel."

"Oh, you don't fuck them, they fuck you. Hard."

I waved my hands in front of my face. "Okay, this just moved into awkward territory."

Faline laughed, just as there was a knock on the door. "Could you grab that? I just have to touch up my make up."

I wobbled my way to her front door, cursing the stilettos heels for making me feel like a fucking giraffe, and opened it. I found Sawyer standing on the other side, dressed in black slacks and a black-button down… in other words, how he normally dressed. His hair had that sexy tousled look, the stubble on his jaw just the other side of five o'clock shadow. Unable to help myself, I drew his chocolate and whisky scent into my nose.

"I see you went all out for tonight," I told him.

His heated gaze raked over my body, and I made sure to stand still. I wasn't going to be intimidated by him. But holy hell. The look in his eyes was electrifying.

"That's what you're wearing tonight?" he asked, almost angrily.

I folded my arms protectively over my chest. "Yes. Why?"

His scorching gaze returned to my face. "No reason. I'm just glad I'm going in armed."

16

Slayke was loud and oppressive. As soon as I set foot inside the door, my opal warmed against my skin and I became hyperaware of the shard of conduit glass sitting in my jacket pocket. While Sawyer spoke to someone he knew, I took a moment to take stock of the club. It was located downtown in a former industrial part of Buxton that had recently undergone a series of upgrades. Trendy bars and clubs had opened there in the last few years, the memories of drug deals and murders a not-too-distant memory.

The outside of Slayke was black brick, but the inside was a combination of deep reds, golds, and black. To our right was the bar. The left side had the DJ booth, elevated above the whole club. Cages hung from the ceiling, but the occupants locked in there didn't look like they wanted to come out any time soon. There were at least two people in each, sometimes three, and there was one that was at least twelve feet by six feet—big enough to house the orgy that was taking place.

I let out a shallow breath and tried to remember that I was here for Faline. That it was her birthday. It wasn't like I was a prude. I enjoyed sex. A lot. It was the mix of human-looking and non-human looking sexual partners in those cages that made me cautious. There was a woman with shimmering purple skin and a long swishy tail dressed as a Dominatrix inside one, with a creature that looked like it had hooves for feet and was covered in hair. It was very clearly male and very clearly enjoying himself.

"Where's everyone else?" I asked, looking around for the rest of the team. Although Brax wasn't coming, that still left BDSM and Growling Guy.

The succubus pouted. "They bailed. It doesn't matter though. Let's go and get a drink!" she shouted above the noise, grabbing my hand and leading me toward the bar. I ordered a double shot of Jack and downed it before ordering another one.

Sawyer sidled up beside me. "See anything you like?" he asked.

I narrowed my eyes at him, then looked out at the crowd. "It's all very… uninhibited."

He laughed. "It's a supernatural sex club. What else did you expect?"

"Touché." I shrugged. "I don't know. I guess I just expected things to be a little more closed door, you know? They could go to a room if they wanted to fuck."

"You can do that too, but the cages are for the exhibitionist and voyeurs. Everyone's needs are catered to here."

"Have you ever been in the cage?" I asked softly. I wasn't sure I wanted to know the answer. When he looked at me again, his eyes were black. He blinked rapidly a few times, the color swirling back to gray.

"Were you just feeding?"

He nodded. "Sorry. It's really fucking hard to ignore the atmosphere in here."

I knew what he was talking about. Sex was like a haze in here, and even though it shouldn't have affected me, I felt my body respond to the sounds and smells around me.

"Does that disgust you?" Sawyer asked, brushing his knuckles gently down my cheek.

I stared at him, holding back the shiver his touch had elicited. "Not as much as I thought it would." Swallowing a mouthful of liquor, I added, "What happens if you don't feed?"

Leaning his elbow on the bar, he drew in a deep breath. "What happens if you don't breathe?" he countered.

"You *have* to do it? Doesn't that get boring?"

"Sometimes," he admitted, "But that's my nature. You can't be angry at something that's built into your DNA."

I grunted and gave him a pass. I guessed he was right. "So, tell me something else, Sawyer."

He turned his body more fully towards me, and I got to check him out a little more. I knew he was wearing the same thing he normally wore to work, but somehow, in this setting, it was all different. He looked edgier, sexier…and I derailed my thoughts right there. I could admit Sawyer was a walking wet dream that made my ovaries go weak, but I couldn't ever go there…could I? Surely that was against workplace rules. Plus, you know, he was a supernatural and an incubus. I'd never know for sure what I was getting from him. Would he always coax the lust from me because that was in his nature, or did he allow these feelings to surface naturally?

"Why are you looking at me like I'm a math problem?"

"Not a math problem. A sex problem."

His brows hit his hair line. "Excuse me?"

I was forced a step closer when a guy the size of a bear shuffled up to the bar, shoving me in the back. "I'm just wondering how you deal with relationships."

"I don't do relationships, so I never have to deal with them."

"Never? You're a one-night stand kind of guy?"

He smiled with all of his teeth. "That's all I ever can be. Incubi and succubi are cursed with the ability to make their partners experience the best sex of their lives, but we're also cursed with never being able to experience anything more than sex. We're also unable to have sex with the same partner more than once." He lowered his head, until our faces were only a few inches apart. I blamed the loud music and general sardines-in-a-can feel of the club, but a jolt of lust streaked through me. "No emotional connection. No longevity. We fuck someone, and we're done. Then we look for something else."

"That sounds lonely."

He jerked away from me. "It is what it is. You can't change your height. At conception, you were designed to be five foot three."

I slugged him in the arm. "I'm five four. Don't deny me my inch."

He grinned. "My point is, you were destined to be short. DNA. You can't mess with it. But my DNA won't allow me to form any sort of emotional connection." He shifted his gaze down to the beer bottle in his hand. "No matter how much we want that to change."

"Wait. Are you trying to tell me there are no incubi in loving, monogamous relationships out there?"

"You sound disappointed, Cat." I flipped him off, and he sighed. "Yes, that's what I'm saying."

I looked back out at the crowd, wondering how I'd feel about that. To only have sex, to have to find a new sexual partner whenever the need arose. Sawyer had to feed and regularly, so he had to blow through at least seven to ten women a week.

A new song began to play, the beat hitting me in the chest with a primal familiarity. I opened my mouth to say as much when all the air got sucked from my lungs, like a concussive wave had just swept through the club, leaving me gasping for O_2. When I could breathe again, I looked around the club to see if anyone else had felt it, but they were all still doing whatever they had been before—drinking, grinding, fucking.

"Dance with me?" Sawyer asked. I looked at him and noticed his eyes were burning black. I nodded, drained my glass, then placed it on the bar with a shaking hand.

He led me into the throng of people, and their bodies bumped against me in a seductive wave. The music was drilling through me, making my lower body clench as erotic whips lashed at me. I looked up at the cage to our right, sucking in a breath when I saw a woman getting fucked from behind while getting a cock shoved into her mouth at the same time. Ménage had always been a fantasy of mine, and I touched the swell of my breasts, drawing my hand down lower.

Sawyer growled low and steady, pressing his body closer to mine, so close that I could feel his erection against my torso. I blinked at him, my head feeling fuzzy and light.

"Your eyes are black," I said, staring into them like they held all the answers to life's greatest mysteries.

"You're turned on right now." His words were a growl.

I nodded, because he was an incubus and he knew. He *knew* what my body was doing, how it was reacting, and right now, my pussy was flooding with liquid heat. Swaying my hips, I tried to get even closer to him.

"We're in a sex club," I pointed out.

Lowering his mouth to my ear, he nipped the lobe, biting down until I gasped in pleasure. "I know. I also know I want to fuck you against the wall right now."

"Why bother moving to a wall when you could do it right here?" I asked, boldly reaching down and stroking him through his pants.

He hissed and threw his head back, his Adam's apple bobbing

as he swallowed. I squeezed my legs together to ease the pain, the throb, the demand my body was making. My abdomen felt heavy, like it was being simultaneously pulled at, teased, and stimulated.

I looked down between us, the sight of my hand on his cock making me shiver. I wanted to drop to my knees and take him into my mouth, to let him do whatever he wanted to me. I didn't care about the audience. I felt liberated and wanton and…

"Fuck," I hissed as he rubbed my pussy through my leather pants. I suddenly wished I'd chosen the dress Faline had first put on. At least that way, Sawyer would have his fingers inside my panties right now instead of rubbing me on top of them.

He kissed my jaw. "Are you wet for me, pussy cat?"

I nodded. "You know I am." I arched my back, begging for more, searching for the friction he could give me.

He drifted his mouth lower, licking the length of my throat before kissing me. His tongue dueled with mine, pushing me higher and higher. I clutched at his arms, then hooked my leg around his waist, his erection finally hitting me where I needed it to be. Moaning, writhing, fucking riding him like he was the only thing anchoring me to this place, I came. I screamed his name, but Sawyer stole the air from my lungs, stole the words from my throat as he pumped against me.

I groaned when he picked me up, wrapped my other leg around his waist and walked me to the wall he mentioned fucking against. Holy shit. With my back plastered against the brickwork, all I could see was him. His normally gray eyes had darkened to a black, stormy tempest, and I could've sworn lightning flashed in their depths.

Slowly, he reached up and slid his fingers along my neck, anchoring his fingers at the base of my skull. His cock pressed against my belly, and he brushed his mouth to mine.

I cried out as another orgasm surfaced so quickly and so strongly that I was glad I wasn't actually using my legs. I felt like I was lit up from the inside, chasing away the darkness of the club.

Sawyer pressed me against the wall, subjecting me to the feel of his arousal. Not that that was such a hardship. Twelve inches indeed. He kissed me again, plunging his tongue into my mouth over and over again. It was an all-out assault, and I needed more. Fisting his shirt, I unashamedly rubbed myself against him like a cat, and he chuckled. It was like satin and daggers—tempting yet so, *so* dangerous.

Sliding one of his hands up under the tank top, he teased my nipples, pinching and rolling them between his finger and thumb. I almost came again then, grinding hard against his cock. He rolled his hips into mine, rocking against me in a rhythm that made me squeeze my eyes shut. Then, I came again.

Panting, I looked at him, wondering why in the hell I hadn't fucked an incubus before. Although, fucking was a stretch. We were both fully clothed. He was just getting me off and doing it spectacularly well.

"Sawyer," I breathed, tucking my head between his neck and

shoulder. I kissed him over his pulse-point, which was roaring against my mouth, then nipped him gently with my teeth. He hissed.

"*Fuck!*" The word sounded as if it had been wrenched from his throat, and he jerked away from me, dropping my legs. Stumbling back a step, he stared at me, the muscles in his neck cording with sudden tension.

"Sawyer?" I asked, staying where I was, because I was pretty sure the wall was holding me up right now. I wiped my mouth with the back of my hand. "What's wrong?"

The black was chased from his eyes, clearing to that familiar cool gray. They darted down to my throat as he swallowed convulsively. "Your necklace…"

The darkness began to bleed back into his irises, and he squeezed his eyes shut. The muscles in his jaw jumped as he clamped it shut. When he opened his eyes again, they were gray, but not the cool, clear gray I was used to. This time, there were like steel.

"It's glowing," he spat out, the effort to speak evident by the lines branching out from the corners of his eyes and bracketing his mouth. At his sides, he balled his hands into fists, flexing them like he was spoiling for a fight…or to stop himself from reaching for me again.

I glanced down, blinking at the bright glow I hadn't noticed until now. Given we were in a dark club, that should've been pretty fucking evident. How had I not noticed that? The skin around the stone was red and raw, my nerve endings finally firing and my brain registering the agony of the burn. Wrapping my fingers around the opal, I sucked in a hiss.

I looked at Sawyer, whose eyes had lightened to pale gray once more. Shutting his lids, he shook his head. He appeared to be as confused as I was…at least, I hoped it was confusion. If it was regret, well, I didn't want to think about that.

As I gripped the opal, more and more of that sex haze lifted, and more and more of the heat bled from the stone. Frowning, I demanded, "What the hell just happened?"

"I don't know. I swear, I don't… Jesus, I'm sorry, Cat."

Folding my arms protectively across my chest, I asked, "What happened?"

"I think…" He rubbed the back of his neck, peering up at me from under his thick lashes. "I think we were under the effect of a spell."

"Say what now?"

"A spell meant just for us."

"How was that…no, you know what? Don't answer that." Good God, I was wet. "You gave me three orgasms," I told him, slightly affronted.

"Do you want me to apologize for that?" he all but growled, and because he was angry, I got angry too.

"I'm sorry if touching me is so repulsive." As I stalked away to find the bathroom, I tried to focus on what he'd said. Someone had bespelled us—and only us—but why? To distract us? To tempt us into fucking each other? I couldn't figure out the why, but I knew how I could.

Locking myself in the first bathroom stall, I shut the lid of the toilet and eased myself down onto it. The last threads of lust were still clinging onto me, and I hoped they disappeared soon. I felt used and somehow dirty. I'd been rubbing up against him like a freaking cat in heat. How was I supposed to look him in the face again? We hadn't just crossed a line; we'd almost had public sex on it.

Pulling the shard of mirror from the pocket of my jacket, I stared at my reflection for a moment, an image that showed a woman whose world had been fucking *rocked* by an incubus not two minutes before. Why the hell had the witch even given this to us, and why had I given up my own blood for it? I touched the vampire bite on my neck, my reflection doing the same. I sighed, and was about to put the shard away, when the image went to black. Frozen, I held onto the mirror so hard that my fingers sliced open and blood welled. I couldn't seem to care as the black melted away to reveal a street. Cars drove by and rain fell. I was seeing through the eyes of the vampire who had made those children.

There was someone walking beside them, and I could see flashes of hair every now and then. It was black from what I could see, but it was also nighttime, so the hair could've also been brown. I blinked when the club came into view. The red neon tubing above the door said Slayke, and when the pair stepped inside, I realized this was real time. The same bouncer when we walked in was there. They walked around the bloated dancefloor, and I gripped the toilet roll holder as they moved down the hallway that led to the bathrooms.

Whoever's eyes I was seeing through stopped at the mouth of the hallway, but the person they were with continued on. And I cursed when I saw who it was.

17

The bathroom door was pushed open, then the lock snicked into place.

"Cat?" Faline called. "Are you in here, babe?"

I glanced around the stall, looking for something I could use as a weapon. But that was the thing with toilet stalls—there wasn't much around that *could* be used… unless I wanted to touch the grimy toilet brush, which I did not. Instead, I put on my big girl panties—unicorn ones, naturally—and replied, "Yeah. I'll be out in a minute."

I unlocked the stall door and stepped out to find Faline leaning against the sink. The dress she'd ended up deciding on was blood red, no doubt to match her mouth. I didn't want to believe she was tangled up in this shit, but evidence didn't lie.

Pretending everything was cool, I washed my hands and dried

them. "Enjoying your birthday?" I asked. "I bet you've been feeding like it's Sizzler."

She smiled, flashing her fangs. "I do love coming here."

"Come on, let's go to the bar and get you a drink." I was hedging badly so far, and I had no doubt she saw straight through me. But the succubus smiled and walked to the door.

"I'd love to, but I'm afraid your night is over, Cat McKenzie," she said, a look of genuine hate in her eyes. I didn't know what I did to deserve that hate, but I was sure she'd tell me. All the bad guys spilled their guts eventually. They couldn't handle not getting the recognition for their evil deeds.

"How did you do it?" I asked.

She smiled again, only this time, it was sinister. And creepy AF. "Clever girl."

I buffed my nails on my shirt. Her shirt. Whatever. "I am clever. And if I figured it out, you can bet your ass Sawyer did too."

"Oh, the same Sawyer who is fucking anything with ovaries out there on the dancefloor right now? Yes, the spell may have worn off completely for you, but Sawyer is now in a frenzy, just as I planned he would be. An incubus who's been denied a release will start looking for sex right away, and he won't stop until he's rendered unconscious, either by the loss of bodily fluids or by someone knocking him out. Since Sawyer is well known here, they wouldn't knock him out just yet. They'd let him have his fill."

I shook my head, a croaked "No" escaping my throat.

Faline laughed. "Poor little human girl sucked into the snare of the incubus. It isn't the first time, and it won't be the last. Who can resist a sex demon after all?"

"Why?" I bit out the word. "Why are you doing this?"

"Because my lover told me to do it. Because he's given me the chance to stop fucking around and be with only one male without getting sick and dying. Because he has given me everything I want."

I snorted. "You sound like a pussy." I was playing for time, although if what she said about Sawyer was true, then I was going to have a hell of a time getting out of here alone.

Faline's expression hardened. "Come on, Cat. You're only prolonging the inevitable."

"Nah, I just like hearing you talk," I told her sweetly. "How do you think you're going to get me out of here without anyone noticing?"

She pulled something out from between her cleavage, something about the size of a golf ball that glowed blue. She blew on it gently, and the ball disintegrated into dust, which covered me completely. I tried to brush it off, but whatever it was, it clung to my skin like ink.

"This is a blending in spell. It will make you all but disappear. It tricks the brain into seeing what they think is there, rather than what is there," she said, preening. "So, you can either walk out on your own two feet, or I can knock your ass unconscious and remove you that way."

"Tough one, but I think you'd rather I remain awake for this, isn't that right? If I'm staring at the back of my eyelids, you'll have to wait until I come around again and that's time you don't have, considering it's already midnight and your vampy lover will probably die at sunrise."

She snarled, baring her fangs at me. "You just have all the answers, don't you?"

"I try."

Taking me by the arm, she wrenched it around behind me, then grabbed my other arm. I struggled to break her hold, but she was much stronger than me. Something cold and hard snapped around one of my wrists, causing panic to bloom and flood my nervous system with all those great human physiological reactions to fear.

"What are you doing?"

My question was chased by the sound of the other cuff closing around my wrist. And that was when I hit my limit. I yanked at the cuffs, the sharp, cold edges cutting into more than just my skin.

"I have no idea how you *think* you're going to get me out of here without anyone noticing me screaming—"

She threw her hand over my mouth, tutting me when I tried to bite her palm. "Don't you worry about a thing," she crooned into my ear, rimming the shell of my ear with her freakishly long tongue. I jerked away as far as I could, causing her to laugh. Yeah, I was a regular comedian. "Come on. Draco is waiting for you."

She unlocked the bathroom, and I opened my mouth to start

screaming. Just as the words were about to come out of my mouth, it felt like a gag was placed between my teeth, even though Faline hadn't put one there.

"A muzzle to keep you quiet," she purred, dragging me down the hallway. When we stepped into the club, I searched frantically for Sawyer, praying what the bitch had told me about him wasn't true. I stumbled to a stop when I found him fucking some random female up against a wall, while a line of more women waited their turn.

"I told you. He needs to exhaust himself, and I knew that spell would work on him. This…" She motioned to Sawyer, but I hadn't taken my eyes off him. "This is what his true nature is."

He was fucking the female he was with but staring at the next one in line. He beckoned her closer and burrowed his free hand up her short dress. A second later, the female's head tilted back against the wall as she shuddered with ecstasy. A pang of longing, regret, and anger went through me, the strange combination of emotions making me feel physically ill.

She dragged me away, through the doors, and outside into the pouring rain. I shivered at the change in temperature, then froze when the vampire Faline was serving stepped from the shadows.

He approached me, wearing his black suit and tie like it was a second skin. His dark hair was slicked back from his face, and I wasn't sure if it was the rain that had done that, or whether it was his regular style. He looked me up and down with dark as pitch eyes, his cruel mouth turning into a sneer at his eyes returned to my face.

"I expected more," he said dismissively, "especially given who your parents were."

I lunged for him, biting back the hiss when Faline yanked back on my wrists. My elbows and recovering dislocated shoulder screamed with the pressure, and I eased back a step. "Don't speak a word about my parents," I snarled.

My statement made him laugh. "Why shouldn't I? I was there when they both died…by my hand."

I blinked at him just as the opal around my neck pulsed with heat. It wasn't glowing though, so the thing was malfunctioning, or it didn't work as I thought it did. Either way, I was fucked.

"Where are you taking me?"

"Why would I tell you?" he shot back. "You think I'm going to reveal all my secrets like some bad Bond villain?"

"I was hoping you would, yes."

He cupped my cheek, making me jerk away with a hiss. His hands were ice-cold. "You have much to learn, Cat McKenzie."

He walked to a town car and popped open the rear door. "Get her in and let's go."

Faline unceremoniously shoved me into the back seat, then slammed the door. I shuffled along uncomfortably, the position of my arms behind my back preventing me from even a sliver of comfort. My shoulder was aching now, and I cursed myself for going out without the sling.

"Someone really should put my seatbelt on," I said when Faline got into the driver's seat and Count Fuckula got in the other side. He turned around to look at me.

"I don't care if you get injured in a car accident, but be a dear and sit behind Faline. A trip through the windshield wouldn't be pleasant."

Grumbling, I slid over. A) because I wasn't stupid, and B) because I had to keep an eye on the bigger threat.

The car glided smoothly over road as the backstabbing succubus navigated away from downtown and out into the wealthier suburbs that had shot up over the last couple of years. Mansions perched on man-made hills, each neighbor trying to outdo the other both in grandiosity and positioning. Really, it was just a very expensive dick measuring contest.

And why was I not surprised when Faline pulled into the driveway of a house that looked like it was the biggest badass on the block?

"I think you could've made it bigger," I told Draco. He glared at me, and I tipped my chin in the direction of the house. "You know, all *this is how big my cock is* kind of thing. Oh! And then added a giant neon sign that reads 'Vampire Sleeps Here.'"

His glare became arctic—not figuratively, but literally. Ice formed on the inside of the windows and on the seats.

"Touchy."

"Shut it, McKenzie," Faline snarled.

I shook my head. "Nope. Sorry. You don't get to have a say in anything I do anymore, Faline. You are on my shit list."

She snarled softly under her breath but didn't take her eyes off the task at hand, which was landing this motherfucking car like it was a jet. Did she think she was driving a truck?

"What's the turning radius like on this thing?" I asked before I was slammed back in my seat forcefully. My head rocked as my brain splashed back in the cranial fluid. My mouth throbbed, and I tongued a cut on my bottom lip. Faline was shaking out her hand. The bitch had hit me, but I hadn't even seen her move.

"You know, your mother was mouthy too," Draco said softly, turning his dark eyes to me. "She didn't stay that way for very long."

Fire erupted in my belly. "What do you know about my mother?"

Yes, I was angry, but not because this bastard had killed her. Okay, I was totally pissed that he'd killed her, but what bugged me more was that he knew she had a smart mouth. Even *I* didn't know that. I didn't remember my mother, which was fucking weird since I was nine when she disappeared, but my father had never been around long enough to talk about her. I felt like her memory had died somehow, and I mourned the loss of knowledge.

"I know that you look *awfully* like your mother, except I think you have your father's nose. She was also very adept with a crossbow."

A crossbow? "I don't understand."

Faline finally brought the town car into land and shut off the engine. "Your parents were members of Rogue Faction," she threw casually over her shoulder, then got out. I blinked, then blinked once more before my eyes dried out. Had she just said

Rogue Faction? Who in the actual fuck were they? She opened the passenger door and reached in, pulling me unceremoniously out of the car. I landed with a *thud* on the pea gravel.

"Watch it," I growled, indicating the tiny pebbles under my ass. "This shit gets into every crevice, especially into the tread of shoes. How annoying is that sound on tiled floors?"

Faline's glower told me she didn't agree, but I maintained my opinion. Draco was already moving with a preternatural, almost gliding grace up the stairs and into the foyer of the house. Faline hauled me up and shoved me hard up the stairs. I stumbled, going down onto one knee. The resounding *pop* echoed around the marble foyer I landed in, and pain streaked through the joint. She picked me up, forcing me to march forward. Every step was agony as the joint threatened to give way.

"I don't suppose I can get some ice?" I asked.

"You'll be lucky to survive the night," she replied.

I tried to ignore her words, but the way my stomach twisted into a hard knot said my brain didn't believe it.

She pushed me down the basement steps, not bothering to catch me as I fell. I tumbled, falling hard on my right shoulder, the same one that was still healing from when my truck got totaled. Biting my lip, I kept the scream in until blood flooded my mouth. I spat it onto the floor of the landing, glowering defiantly at Faline as she stepped behind me.

"Oops," she said.

I'd give her *oops*. I shuffled around until I was on my knees, well, just one knee. I held the other one off the ground, since the pain was too much to bear if there was any weight on it.

"What are you going to do to me?"

She looked over my shoulder, and I followed her gaze, sucking in a gasp when I saw what was there. On a raised platform that looked like a metal table you found at a vet clinic, was a coffin. Its polished red-brown mahogany surface reflected back the bare bulb hanging overhead. I swallowed.

"Is that where Lover Boy sleeps?" I asked, hoping she didn't hear the shake in my voice.

"No. That's where you're going to sleep. Forever."

She physically picked me up this time, threw open the casket's lid, and dumped me facedown into the cold white satin. My panic was instant. It felt like barbed wire was winding around my chest, squeezing tighter and tighter with every beat of my heart. My shoulder throbbed in time with my pulse, my knee an accompanying base line. With my elbows locked and both shoulders screaming at the position, I knew I was going to have to get some serious chiropractic help after I got out here.

"Why are you doing this, Faline?" I asked when I was sure my breath was steady. "I thought we were friends."

Her responding laugh was derisive. "Oh, that's so sweet. You thought that, huh?"

"Yes," I ground out. "Why?"

"Because of who you are." Draco's voice sounded far away, but as he spoke, it got closer. "Because you are the last of your lineage."

"Last of what lineage?"

"Your parents' marriage was the linking of the two strongest Rogue Faction blood lines in the world, and *your* birth was a physical manifestation of that that link. You have so much power flowing inside your veins, but you have no idea how to harness it."

I choked down his words, finding them sharp and uncomfortable. "I've never heard of an organization called Rogue Faction before."

"That's because I've made it my job for the last five years to eradicate every single last one of them," he screamed suddenly, losing the face of his civility.

I turned my face on the satin pillow to look at him as he stood over the casket.

He leaned in and whispered conspiratorially, "This is where you say, 'You'll never get away with this.'"

"I'm not misquoting *Scooby-Doo* for you," I replied, sucking in a hiss when my shoulder screamed at the shift in position. "You made all the baby vampires. Why?"

He smiled, flashing his fangs. "To draw you out, to see what you were made of. I wanted to know whether you were a worthy adversary like your father was… before I killed him. Did you know he begged me not to kill you after I was done with him? He begged me and begged me to let you go, to live. He also promised he'd leave the Faction if I let you both go. That he'd disappear with you and I'd never hear from him again."

A tear squeezed from the corner of my eye. "Why are you telling me this?"

"Because I want you to know that about him before I kill you like he killed my kiss."

So, this is why he was doing this. "How many did he kill?"

"All of us," he replied, a haunted look on his face. "My family, the one I'd built for two centuries, was just gone in a flash of fire."

"I'd say I'm sorry, but I'm not."

His expression clouded over. "Neither was your father until I caught up with him in Turkey. He was clearing out another kiss with such zealous fervor that I recognized in him what I was feeling. Your mother died on that mission when she destroyed my kiss, and then your father was hell-bent on destroying every vampire he could find in order to avenge her.

"What he didn't know was that I was on a similar mission. I hunted them all down, and he was last of his team. He was the one I wanted the most, because he was the one who gave the order to destroy everything." He turned his sharp, dangerous eyes to me. "Do you want to know how he and his team killed my family? They wrapped their coffins in silver, then set them alight. They were roasted in there, unable to get out because of your father."

It dawned on me then why I was in this fucking coffin. "I think you're taking this a little too far," I said, my mind scrambling to come up with a way out of this. "You could just kill me if you want to kill me. Stop with the theatrics."

He chuckled, but it sounded dead. "Where's the fun in that? Vampires are nothing if not theatrical." He turned to walk away, but paused and faced me once more. "Oh, and your partner, the one I took while you stood there like a dolt? His fear was the best I'd tasted… well, next to your father's, of course."

He had killed my partner?

And just like that, I was dragged back to one week ago…

It was a dark night, and we were investigating a call about someone trespassing in a junkyard. We were walking back after making sure the fence was secure, when my partner screamed. Harrold was his name. He screamed, and then the sound was cut off. I'd spun around, my flashlight jumping spasmodically around the old cars, damaged and broken appliances, and scrap metal that was piled up around me. I couldn't see him… all I could do was *hear* him. Terror gripped me by the throat, strangling any sounds I would have made…

And then I froze.

I simply turned off the flashlight, shut my eyes, and prayed for Harrold to stop taking those rattling, gasping exhalations.

I blinked rapidly, trying to erase the sounds of my first partner's final breaths from my memory. "He was a good man," I growled. "He had a family."

"He was a human. Disposable. Besides, he was a means to an end. His death got you transferred to PIG, where my darling Faline worked."

My gaze jumped to her face as she stared down at me. "You knew who I was?"

"The moment you breezed through the door," she replied. Reaching up, she shut the lid of the coffin, leaving me with nothing but darkness and the screaming in my head. My breathing was an erratic wheeze through my mouth, the humid air I was producing soon making the interior of the coffin even more claustrophobic than it already was.

Forcing myself to calm down, I took shallower breaths, trying to focus on something other than my impending death. I strained my ears, listening for any movement, any tell-tale sound around me, but the satin and thick wood dampened the sound. My only chance to escape would be when they opened the casket again… *if* they opened the casket again. Knowing my shitty luck, they were already building a fire under this thing and getting the marshmallows ready.

I shifted a little, then paused when I felt something long and hard settle between my shoulder blades. I inhaled, taking in the slight tinge of old leather, then breathed a sigh of relief. Reaver was here… somehow. Honestly, after this, I was going to let the sword sleep in my bed if it wanted to. But how was I supposed to use it with my hands tied behind my back?

Then I remembered…

It would mean binding myself to magic—something I'd sworn I'd never do—but if I didn't, the only thing I'd be doing in the future would be feeding the worms. I rubbed my thumb along the inside of my hand, feeling the cuts on my fingers. I just hoped the wounds I'd inflicted on the conduit mirror hadn't coagulated too much. Wrapping my hand gently around the bare blade, I sucked in a hiss as I reopened those cuts. Immediately, Reaver grew warmer under my touch, the steel throbbing in time with my racing pulse. Beneath me, the opal also began to glow as Reaver's magic poured through me, but the stone flickered a few times before finally extinguishing.

A vibration started coming from the sword, transferring into my body as the frequency increased. It became uncomfortably strong, and I tried to release my fingers from the blade, but I couldn't let go. Reaver was stuck to my skin, and I grit my teeth against the onslaught. Blood and magic was a dangerous combination, a combination I wouldn't have ever found out about if I wasn't about to be murdered by a psycho vampire.

The marrow in the bones of my hands, arms, and shoulders quaked as the shivering steel intensified to the point of pain. Gritting my teeth, I screamed into the pillow, writhing in place. After the longest minute of my life, something cold fell against my side, and I realized the cuffs had fallen away. My arms fell to my sides, the ache in my shoulders acute.

I curled my fingers around Reaver's hilt, the sword now down at waist level. This fucking blade would creep me out if it wasn't saving my life.

With my hands unbound and a weapon at my disposal, my fear and anxiety started to ebb away, leaving cold hate and a determination to survive in its place. I steadied my breathing, taking longer and longer breaths to focus my mind. Someone came down the stairs again, and judging by the clack of heels, it was Faline. Quickly, so she wouldn't think anything was amiss, I placed my hands behind my back and rolled onto my side as she opened the casket lid.

Her dark hair was disheveled, but her green eyes were bright. The smell of sex perfumed the air, and I screwed my face up.

"You just fucked the cadaver?" I asked. "He's as cold as the grave."

She flashed the inside of her wrist. "Not after he's fed, he's not. With my blood pumping through his veins, he's warm and hard and ripe for the plucking."

"Don't say the word *hard* to me." I shuddered. "I get a mental image."

She folded her arms and stared at me. Like I was a puzzle. Which I guessed I was, given I was so fucking ignorant of what my parents did for a living and I had a magical sword following me around like a dog.

"You'll be dying in an hour. Any last words?"

An hour? This was probably my last chance to get out of here. "Yeah. Why the fuck would you delay this shit?"

Her nostrils flared. "He wants to wage psychological warfare on you. He wants to make you sweat. After all, revenge is a dish best served cold."

"Well, you can let him know he's doing an exceptional job of that." I wrapped my fingers around Reaver's hilt—the fingers of my left hand because my right shoulder was fucked—and let out a breath. "Do me a favor though?" I said. "Can you just scratch my nose for me?"

"What?"

Rolling my eyes theatrically, because why should Draco have all the thespian fun, I said, "I have an itch. On my nose. You cuffed me. I can't reach it."

With a long-suffering growl, she leaned down to scratch my fictional itch, and that was when I made my move. Bringing my arm up in a cumbersome arc, I brought Reaver down onto her neck, slicing through it with very little effort. Her head bounced off my chest, landing face-down between me and the side of the casket. Blood gushed from her neck, filling the inside of the coffin. The white satin turned red, eagerly absorbing the hot liquid. Bile hit the back of my throat.

Before I could talk myself out of it, I grabbed Faline by the hair and threw her head out of the casket, blood spiraling like macabre confetti around her. The appendage landed with a dull *thud*, and I vomited, emptying my stomach both onto me and into the coffin. After the gagging stopped, I sat up, sucking in another hiss as my right shoulder reminded me with agony-filled fingers that shit was not okay in the scapular region of my body.

Wiping a hand over the back of my mouth, I peered over the edge of the casket to make sure Faline was good and dead. If I'd learned anything from horror movies and *The Walking Dead*, it was that things rarely came back from decapitation. When there was movement above my head, I jerked to look at the ceiling and cursed—*softly*, because vampire. Hauling myself onto my good knee, I eased myself out of the coffin and off the edge of the table, making sure to keep my grip on Reaver tight. I skirted around the growing puddle of blood from Faline and began looking for somewhere to hide. The only problem was there was *nowhere* to hide. This guy had the cleanest fucking basement I'd ever seen. Who the hell did he think he was, Marie Kondo?

The basement door opened then, and I bolted under the stairs.

Draco's steps were light, almost non-existent, but he couldn't control the air he displaced as he moved. From my vantage, I saw him reach the landing and freeze. I could only see him in profile, but his expression was twisted into genuine grief. I should've known he'd felt the moment I ended Faline's life. He walked over to the casket and flipped off the lid, then hissed when he realized I was gone.

Easing out from under the stairs, I readjusted my grip on Reaver and hesitated. I hesitated because I could just as easily run up those stairs, out of the basement and away…but vampires were fast. I'd seen that, so standing and fighting also seemed like a good idea. Cut the head off the snake and all that.

"I don't think you can return that coffin now," I said, hoping I sounded as brave out loud as I did in my head. Draco spun around in a whoosh of tailored suit and snarled.

"You killed her."

I dipped my chin. "At least you aren't blind."

"How?"

I looked down to find Reaver gone. Again. I glanced back up at him and shrugged. "Call me resourceful."

"I'll call you dead," he said on a snarl as he launched himself at me. I braced for impact, widening my stance. He hit me with what felt like five hundred pounds of muscle and anger, but I rolled with it, absorbing the hit and toppling over. Taking this to the ground was a mistake, but I had to trust that Reaver knew what it was doing.

And now I was talking like Reaver had a brain and made tactical decisions.

My head slammed back into the bare concrete floor when Draco's fist collided with my face. I blinked the black fuzzies out of my eyes, trying to focus on where the next strike was coming from. He caught me in the mouth, popping open my split lip that had barely healed. By the time I was done here, I was afraid of what the doctors at the hospital would think of me.

Draco's fist hovered above me, and I dodged the strike, making the bastard punch the concrete instead. He hissed, blood leaking from his shattered hand. I was horrified to learn that vampires didn't sustain damage like regular people. The mangled mess of bones in his hand knitted back together right before my eyes.

"Son of a bitch," I breathed.

I scrambled to get out from under him, finally breaking free and jumping up. He grabbed me by the back of my jacket, and I let my arms slide through so all he was left with was red leather. I bolted for the stairs, rethinking my earlier dumbass logic. Nope, this time, I was going to fucking bolt and hide until the sun came up.

Then I might come back here for a lunchtime cookout. Was it still considered murder if they were already dead?

I only made it up half a dozen stairs before he snagged my foot. I jammed the heel backwards, cringing at the squelch as the stiletto heel went straight through his eye. He released me long enough for me to scramble up another two steps before he tackled me back to the ground. I grunted as I fell, attempting to suck back in the breath that was knocked from me.

I propelled myself up another few steps, kicking wildly as I went. A cut opened up on his cheek when I swiped at his face, but it healed almost instantly. Up and up we went, playing this strange game of cat and mouse, only the victor of this game got murder added to their tally.

When I reached the top of the stairs, I went through the door, just not in the way I expected. Draco launched himself at me, landing on my back and riding me to the kitchen floor the basement opened on to. Wood splintered as the doorway shattered around us.

"I'm not a fucking unicorn!" I yelled, jerking and jostling, trying to dislodge him. He was strong, but I didn't think he was at full strength. Perhaps Faline's death had weakened him somehow? Whatever the reason, I was fucking grateful. Now all I needed was Reaver to start playing nice.

As Draco flipped me over onto my back, he wrenched my head to the side and tipped my chin up, giving him unfettered access to my throat and the carotid artery that pounded against my skin. Oh, hell no. I was not a juice box. As he leaned in, his mouth open, his fangs growing from tiny points to two-inch monstrosities, I sucked in a breath and braced for my throat to be torn out. I was not, however, braced for the scream that sounded as if it was being forcefully ripped from his vocal cords…with a pair of hot pliers.

My opal had flared back to life, this time holding its glow. It grew in intensity, and whatever it was, whatever it was doing, Draco did not appreciate it. Rearing back, he hissed at me, his features no longer that of a man, but of the monster hidden under his skin. His eyes glowed like hot coals. Black veins erupted all over his skin, raised and pulsing, and his mouth was a terrifying snarl with daggers for teeth.

Shielding his eyes from the glow, he reached blindly for my neck. And that was when I felt Reaver down by my left hand. I clutched at the magnificently mercurial blade and brought it up, swinging it in an arc that cleaved the head from Draco's body. His head landed to my right, his body listed to the left, blood spewing from both appendages and smattering across my chest in an X. It coated my legs and lower torso until I looked as if I'd gone all Carrie on his ass. Which, I guessed, I kind of had.

I sat up with a wince, bringing the blade with me. I stared at it. "You have some of the best and worst timing in the world."

Panting, breathless, I clung to the opal, which had stopped glowing as soon as Draco's head separated from his body. I needed to find out how it worked. I needed a fucking shower. Then a therapy session.

Shit.

Joanna Wong wouldn't know what hit her.

18

I had the good sense to call Wolfe and tell him what had happened. He wasn't too happy to hear from me at three in the morning, but I told him that not having baby vampires running around anymore would be his reward for taking the call. He cursed me out a little, then said he would send a team to the scene.

As I sat in the stainless steel and cherry wood kitchen waiting, I tried to work through everything. The most pressing thing was the secrets my parents had kept from me. I had to find out more, and I had to find out how this opal was connected. I glanced down at Reaver, still coated in blood. My impulse was to clean the thing, but I didn't want to mess with the crime scene any more than I already had.

My right shoulder throbbed, as did the cut on my hand, the

bump on my head, and my knee. These past few days had been a real shit show, but I actually kind of enjoyed them. It sure beat a desk job in any case. I glanced up when I heard the front door open.

"McKenzie?" someone called.

"In the kitchen," I shouted back happily.

Two cops in thick jackets came in and took in the scene, then looked at me. Reaver, conveniently, disappeared. "EMTs are on the way."

"Thanks."

"What the hell happened?"

"Vampire?" I replied.

The first guy, whose nametag said his name was Ramirez, said, "No, I mean how in the hell did you sever someone's head completely? Look at you, you're five foot three."

I glowered. "Five four, douche canoe," I snarled.

Ramirez put his hands up in surrender. "Sorry. Wouldn't want to deny you an inch."

"An inch makes all the difference," I shot back sweetly, looking down at his junk.

He shook his head. "Yeah, yeah." Looking over his shoulder, he said to his partner, "Come on. Wonder Woman here will be okay for a few minutes."

"There's more fun downstairs," I said. "I got a little decapitation happy," I added with a shrug. "Bad habit. I'm going to therapy for it."

The two cops shook their heads and went downstairs. I was

either going to be a fucking badass for killing two supes by decapitation… or I was going to be the freak of nature who killed two supes by decapitation. Either way, I was alive and the bad guys were dead, but the bastards had left me a puzzle to figure out all on my own.

It was only after a few more minutes when I heard the sirens. The EMTs were here, and I was closer to falling into a bed. When they walked into the kitchen, they looked at Draco, then at me.

"He said I was short," I told them with a shrug. One of them blanched a little, then put his professional face on.

Dropping his jump bag onto the counter beside me, he said, "What's your name?"

"Cat."

"Okay, Cat, can you tell me what happened?"

"Where would you like me to start?"

"At the beginning, preferably."

So I did. I saved him the trouble of listening to everything that had happened before the night out. That was just for my therapist to know. I also left out the part about my parents and Draco's reasoning for targeting me specifically. I played dumb when he asked about how I decapitated the big bad vampire, letting them think I was some sort of supernatural with awesome strength. Sometimes, being unassuming was the best way to fuck someone over.

By the time the EMTs were done, the house was crawling with CSI, cataloguing everything they could find. I thought it was kind of stupid actually to have PIG in place for investigating paranormal crimes, but not have a paranormal CSI. What if some things were enchanted or magical in nature, so when they went and touched it, they ended up cursing themselves or killing someone else? Maybe that was something I could bring up with Wolfe when I reported to him tomorrow.

"We're going to take you to the hospital now, Cat. Did you need to collect anything from here?"

I shivered in the blanket they'd given me and shook my head. "I'm ready to leave this house of horrors."

When I arrived at the hospital, I was taken straight to the ER to have my shoulder x-rayed. They were concerned that more damage had been done with the cuffs and wanted a better look at my knee, which had blown up to the size of a grapefruit. They stitched up my hand and gave me a cold compress for my head. By the time I was wheeled onto the ward, the sun was well established in the sky and the clock on the wall read nine-fourteen.

I fell asleep as soon as the wheels were locked in place.

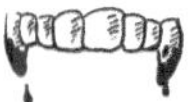

THE NEXT TIME I WOKE, SOMEONE WAS STROKING MY ARM. I PEELED open my eyes to find Sawyer there. He looked hollowed out. Black rings were under his eyes, and all the color had leached from his face. I thought he'd even lost a little weight.

"You're awake."

I nodded. "You are too. Which was it in the end—loss of all

bodily fluids, or did someone knock you out?"

He grimaced and looked away. "The owner of the club eventually knocked me out at closing time. I…" He sighed. "I wasn't myself."

"Is that what normally happens if you're denied?"

He nodded, just once. "It hasn't happened in a very long time."

"I'm sorry then, since I was the one who… ran, I guess."

"You were right to get the hell out of there, Cat. If we'd fucked, things would've been so different."

I shrugged, instantly regretting it. I sucked in a hiss and looked down at the sling keeping my right arm immobile. Sawyer's fingers tightened around my hand.

"Your shoulder will be fine with rest—you didn't dislocate it again, but it did get strained. I'm not sure what other injuries you have. The nurses and doctors aren't too forthcoming with people who aren't immediate family, and since you didn't have a next of kin registered, they're even less willing to talk to me."

"I don't have a next of kin because Draco killed my parents."

"He did what? What the hell happened last night, Cat?"

I stared at him, waiting for any hint that he knew about me, about my past, or about what happened. "My parents were part of an organization called Rogue Faction. Have you heard of them before?"

He frowned. "I'd heard of teams of humans who were believers before we revealed ourselves, but I didn't think they were organized in any particular way. You're saying they were?"

"If what Draco said is true, then yes. They're organized, and if Draco didn't kill them all, there are more of them out there. I tend to take everything a psychopath says with a grain of salt."

"What happened to your parents?"

"When I was ten, my mom just didn't come home from a trip, and when my dad did, he looked dead himself. Apparently, my father went on a killing spree. He was looking for revenge, for absolution. He was clearing out a kiss in Turkey when Draco found him. Draco was the lone survivor of his Italian kiss, and he blamed my father for the slaughter. So he killed him. And he wanted to kill me because *apparently*, I'm a combination of two of the strongest bloodlines in Rogue Faction."

"You?" His brows shot up in disbelief.

I nodded. "Me. Draco wanted me dead, but I didn't give him the satisfaction." I looked around the hospital room. It was nice for someplace sterile and white. "Did you hear about Faline?"

His expression turned stormy, his eyes darkening to nearly black. "I heard. She was working with him?"

"Apparently. Evidently, he promised her she wouldn't become sick and die if she fed exclusively from him. She felt like that was a good deal."

"But she's been a cop for years. I don't understand how she could just switch sides like that."

It was a rhetorical question, but I answered him anyway. "You yourself said you'd give anything to stop this cycle of perpetual loneliness. What if a woman said to you that she could make it all stop? You could stop screwing everything that moved and be happy and healthy with just one female. Would you do it?"

"In a heartbeat," he replied.

"And there's your answer, Sawyer Taylor."

His gaze clearing, it drifted over to Reaver, which was propped up in the other visitor's chair in the corner. It hadn't been there a moment ago.

"Did it show up in time to save you?"

I nodded. "It went away in time to have my ass handed to me too, but it showed up again when it mattered."

My partner's expression vacillated between anguish, guilt, and anger. "I'm so sorry, Cat."

"For what?"

The muscle in his jaw feathered. "For not being there. For not noticing you were gone."

"You were under the influence of a spell."

"That's not an excuse. You broke it…" He looked down at where my opal was sitting against my sternum, hidden by the gown. "You broke through the spell while I was chained to a biological imperative."

"You can't fight your nature, Sawyer." Reaching out slowly, I placed my hand on his. "You're an incubus. Sex is what you need, what you do, what you think, breathe, and eat." I retracted my hand and settled it on my stomach. "I am but a lowly human," I said with a wink.

"You're more than that, Cat, and you know it."

I raised my brows, inviting him to say more. Hey, I was in a hospital room with an aching shoulder, a busted knee, and bruised to the hilt. I could do with a little ego stroking.

"You have no idea, do you? You should've been dead in the principal's office that first day we met. That Renfield was going to kill you."

I was going to shrug, to dismiss his words, but then I thought about it. "I am pretty amazing, right?"

He chuckled. "Yeah, I'd say so."

Silence fell on the room. "Can we link it all to Draco? I mean, does it all fit?"

I thought it did, but Sawyer was better at understanding the supernatural stuff than I was. "I think so. The Renfield in the principal's office was one of his. He was making the baby vampires in order to draw you out, although how he knew you'd be the one..." He paused, then swore.

"What? What is it?"

"Faline."

"Oh, I love this game. Dead." He gave me a look. "You're supposed to say the first word you think of when you hear the word 'dead.'"

Shaking his head, he said, "Faline was supposed to be my partner, not you. About a week before you came strolling into the office, she said she wanted to work alone. I couldn't understand it at the time, because we worked so well together. Now it makes sense. She was engineering it so that you would become my partner."

"None of the other members of PIG have partners," I pointed out.

"That's because they don't play nice," he replied. "Well, except for Brax, but he never goes out into the field. He's more of our secretary."

"I'm going to tell him you said that."

He shook his head. "Faline played me, played us, the whole time."

I thought back to her showing up at my kickboxing class, then at my apartment after the crash. She did seem to just know where I was going to be, popping up at the most convenient time.

"I'm glad she's dead," I said, holding Sawyer's gaze. "I'm glad I killed her. You can't have people you don't trust guarding your back."

He smiled. "You're right about that, Cat."

When Sawyer went to get something to eat and to sneak me in a hamburger, I picked up my phone from the rolling table beside my bed and unlocked it. I had about a gazillion missed calls and texts from Sasha. I began scrolling through, feeling more and more guilty as the simple wording of 'Hey, what's happening?' turned into 'OMFG, WHERE ARE YOU???' toward the end.

I shut down the message app and called her.

"Oh, my fucking god!' she shouted when the call connected. "Why haven't you been answering my calls and texts?"

"Hey, Sash," I said lamely. "I'm really—"

"Don't you dare say sorry," she screeched. Yanking the phone away from my ear, I wondered if she was part banshee and didn't know it. Slowly, like I was bringing a grenade with the pin pulled out back to my head, I listened as she continued her rant.

"…at class, Mike asked about you and you didn't answer my

calls and I thought you were dead and why *the fuck* didn't you answer my calls and texts?"

I cringed. I didn't know how much more of this I could take. When my friend stopped long enough to take a breath, I cut in. "I'm sorry, Sasha. Things got..." Murderous? Nah, too dramatic. Busy? Not dramatic enough. "Things were crazy at work. Long hours. Trips to the hospital. Things like that."

"The hospital? Is that where you are right now?"

I sucked on my teeth for a moment, wondering how much I could tell her without her coming down here. I was getting out soon, and I didn't want her to come all the way down here if I wasn't going to be here for much longer. "Yes?"

Stunned silence.

I soaked it up while I could.

"Yes?? What the fuck happened to you?"

Sighing, I ran my fingertips over the textured blanket around my legs. "I may have gone to a sex club and maybe, kind of gotten into a fight with a succubus and then a vampire?"

"You *may have?*" she retorted.

Yeah, it was a pretty fucking thin excuse. "I did and now he's dead, so all good."

Sasha exhaled sharply, and when she spoke again, her voice was modulated. "Okay. I know you're a cop, Cat, so I knew things like this were going to happen. I'd just hoped that you would've told me about them."

And didn't that just make me feel like shit? I was a terrible friend. "I'd intended to, Sash, but things just got out of control."

This was the first time we'd ever had an argument like this, so I wasn't sure what I could or should say. In the end, I settled for good old-fashioned contrition. "I really am sorry. And I promise I'll keep you in the loop when I can."

She sniffed. "That's all I can ask." There was a beat of silence, then, "So I've met someone…"

I smiled as I listened to Sasha wax lyrical about the dick size of the guy she was dating, how much of a fucking boss he was in the bedroom, and how they were seeing each other again tonight. Although this was a fucked-up conversation to be having with me in the hospital, it did actually make me feel better. I was reconnecting with my friend, and it made me realize how lucky I was to have her.

19

I ended up staying at the hospital for another few days. My knee had a severe bone bruise, leaving me in a brace and regularly icing it for at least a month. In the meantime, I was on light duties, which meant I stayed at my desk for most of the day while Sawyer went out and interviewed people.

I didn't mind it much, until about day three. That's when I started climbing the fucking walls, itching to get out there and solve crimes with my partner. With my partner… I kind of liked the way those words sounded. My prejudice against supes was waning as I learned that, like people, not all of them are a bag of dicks. Some of them were genuinely nice and genuinely likable. The jury was still out on Wolfe though.

So, I spent my days hanging with Brax in between Sawyer's return from interviews or crime scenes. We'd play paper hoops and shoot the shit. It turned out the guy was a member of the local werewolf pack.

"So, how does it work?" I asked one sunny afternoon as I launched a crumpled-up ball of paper left-handed into the recycling bin. "You just get furry once a month?"

"More than once a month if I want to," he replied.

"What color is your fur?"

He pointed to his dark hair. "Same color as this."

"Is your wife a werewolf?"

"Mate, and yes."

"Mate." I tried the word out. "So that means your kids are werewolves too, right?"

"Yep."

I grabbed another piece of scrap paper, crushing it in my palm. "Does it hurt, the shift?"

He nodded. "It's like getting your bones broken, scrambled up, and reset, all while getting an all-over body wax finished off with an acid wash."

"Stop, you're making it sound so fun," I replied, sarcasm heavy in my voice, then grinned. "Do you control the wolf, or does the wolf control you?"

He took another shot, this one bouncing off the edge of the bin. "Ninety-nine percent of the time, I control it. The only time I let go of that control is when I'm running on our pack's land. We can't hurt anyone there, so it's the only place that's safe to do it."

"Do you enjoy being a werewolf?" I took my next shot,

pumping my fist in the air when it landed without hitting the sides.

"I do. It's the best feeling, knowing my pack—my family— have my back no matter what." He took his shot and missed with a curse.

"I wouldn't know what that felt like," I said softly, crushing the paper ball in my fist into a more compact sphere.

"Family?"

I nodded and sat back in my chair. "Yeah. I don't have one anymore."

"Sure you do," he replied. "What do you think we are to you now?"

"Work colleagues?" I hedged.

He made an obnoxious game show buzzer sound. "Forget that, Cat. You're one of us. A family."

"A family of misfits," I shot back with a smile. "But that's okay, because I'm a misfit too."

He laughed and stared pointedly at Reaver, who was laid out on top of my desk. "Yes, you are. I've never met a human followed around by a sword before."

I glanced over at said sword, giving it a soft smile. "It's saved my life a lot these last few days."

"Which is also fucking strange. Do you know where we got Reaver from?" I shook my head. "A fallen angel. Yeah, we stripped it from him when he was processed for a misdemeanor crime about two months ago."

I opened my mouth to ask for more details, then shut it. Some things were better off being mysteries. And some things were better off simply embraced without question. As we played paper hoops, I turned over Brax's words in my head. I was an orphan for all intents and purposes, and now being an adult, that shouldn't have such an impact on me, but as a human, I had needs. Love and protection were what I'd always craved. Mrs. Brown had provided a lot of what my mother could no longer give me, but I thought my father had stopped thinking about me and was solely focused on revenge.

Had I found that love and protection again here at PIG? I smiled to myself and nailed my last shot.

"You owe me a beer," I crowed as I did a shuffled version of my victory dance. Brax only laughed and beaned me with one of his paper balls.

"I'll let you drain the whole damn bar if you stop dancing like that. I can't unsee that now, Cat. Seriously."

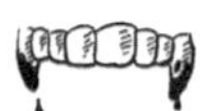

On Friday afternoon, I went to my regular appointment to see Joanna Wong. As I limped into her office, she gave me a wide-eyed look. Once I was settled, she sat down in the armchair opposite me, her notepad balanced on her knee and her pencil at the ready.

"So, how are you feeling today, Cat?"

I grinned. "You are not going to believe the week I've had."

BAD VAMPIRE